My Father's House

A Novella by
Ben Tanzer

MINT HILL BOOKS
MAIN STREET RAG PUBLISHING COMPANY
CHARLOTTE, NORTH CAROLINA

Copyright © 2011 Ben Tanzer

Author photograph (back cover) by Jacob S. Knabb.

Special Thanks to David Masciotra, Mel Bosworth, John Reed and Michael FitzGerald, great friends and writers all. Appreciations to M. Scott Douglass and S. Craig Renfroe, yes, they both have initials in their names, and no, I don't know why this is. But I like it. And big love to my father, Bruce Springsteen, Binghamton, NY and Thirsty's, all of whom, and which, I return to again and again.

Library of Congress Control Number: 2011923700

ISBN: 978-1-59948-293-4

Produced in the United States of America

Mint Hill Books
Main Street Rag Publishing Company
PO Box 690100
Charlotte, NC 28227
www.MainStreetRag.com

For my mom who has been there from the start.

1.

I don't even remember how this started exactly.

I know it was 1999 and I know that my father had a seizure. I know his blood didn't look right. And that there was something going on with his bone marrow that looked to be pre-cancerous, but needed to be confirmed with a genetic test.

I also know it turned out that he has myelodisplasia, a rare form of bone cancer that causes immature bone marrow cells to explode before reaching maturity; that these explosions are known as blasts and without treatment these blasts are going to escalate until he has full-blown Leukemia.

The doctor at Sloan-Kettering says that my dad may have been sick for awhile because his red blood cells looked low as early as last summer. The doctor also said that my dad needs a bone marrow transplant and that the disease is worse then they thought and progressing, though it's just hard to imagine how that's possible.

My mom says people can walk in to see a doctor, hear they have this disease and die three months later. Of course, she also says that people who get bone marrow transplants can live five more healthy years.

The thing is there needs to be a match, and while siblings are the best bet, it turns out that they only match about twenty-five percent of the time. In comparison, children only match about three percent of the time, so they won't even test my brother Jerry and I until they are truly desperate.

Maybe my uncles will be a match. Or maybe it will be Jerry or I. And if it is one of us then maybe they will wheel us into some cold and antiseptic hospital room and put tubes into our lower back and then very slowly draw the bone marrow that could very well save my dad's life.

That would be something wouldn't it?

Sure it would, though this is assuming of course that he doesn't die on the operating table, that his body doesn't then reject the transplant or that some opportunistic infection doesn't wreak havoc on his now compromised immune system.

But let's say that there is a match, and that these things don't happen, who knows what's possible, right? I can feel a little hopeful, can't I? Well, I don't actually know that anyone would quite say that, because I don't know that anyone really knows anything, most of all me.

I do know though that I have this image of the old man that I plan to hold on to. I pulled up to the house with my wife Kerri today and when I arrived my father was up on the porch leaning over the rail and tending to his bushes. He was in his ratty old Cape Cod sweatshirt and he was surrounded by all this foliage and shrubbery. It was this brilliant day and he was smiling, all active and healthy looking, tending to his plants, the plants he planted with his bare hands. He looked so peaceful and focused, nothing like he could have looked like, tired and sallow, beat-down and sickly looking. And before I yelled hello I paused to take it all in, my old man, Monet-like, in his garden, relaxed and happy.

It's the image I won't let go of. It's a keeper.

2.

I call Jerry to talk about our dad and we will talk about him, we just won't talk much about what's going on. Jerry doesn't do that.

People joke about how siblings always seem to have somehow grown-up in different homes and yet somehow that usually seems to be the case. Families do change over time. Parents change. Circumstances change. Sometimes its financial, or the outcome of more, sometimes less members. The dynamics are always swirling.

My dad never worried about Jerry. From the start Jerry seemed to know what he was doing and he was treated as such. He could come and go as he pleased and so for him the house was a way station between things and the world he lived in was far removed from the anxieties and tensions that intermittently sprang to life wrapping my mother and I in tendrils that still linger, even if they're more like ghosts now, hovering and watching, if not totally apparent to the naked eye.

There is one association with growing-up that we hold in common though, and it is always something we can focus on when other topics are too difficult to tackle. Our dad was from New York and he thought of himself as a tough guy.

"So, this one time," I say to Jerry about to repeat an oft told story of my dad's legendary toughness, "dad and this friend of his were up on the roof of his building and its summer and it's real hot, so hot that people are unscrewing the plugs on the fire hydrants so everyone can splash around in the cold water. And the tar on the roof is melting, right?"

"Right, continue" Jerry says even though he has heard and told this story a thousand times.

"Anyway, so the tar is melting, and dad and his friend get this idea that they're going to fill paper bags with the tar and then pelt the windows of police cars as they drive by. And then they do it. And the police try to chase them, but they can't catch them because they run across the rooftops and make their escape."

"Yeah, I know that one," Jerry says before moving on to another story, which I will know, but he will tell anyway, because that's part of the game, "and then there was the time he went to Chinatown with his gang to buy some firecrackers from a rival gang. For some reason the deal went bad and they found themselves running away from the other gang and trying to figure out how they were going to make it home."

"It's funny isn't it," I say.

"What?" Jerry says.

"Dad never seems to notice that every story he tells us involves running away from someone or some situation."

"I don't see what you mean," Jerry says.

"Dad, running away…"

"No, what…look, whatever."

Jerry doesn't really remember the bad stuff, or let himself get angry. I envy that.

"Hey," I say, hoping to get us back on track, "so they're on the run, and then what, what happened next?"

"What happened next," Jerry says, "they threw the cherry bombs at the other gang and stopped them dead in their tracks."

We both laugh.

"And you know that just might be true," I say.

"Yeah, maybe, I hope so," Jerry replies.

We get quiet.

And then we get off of the phone.

3.

I feel like today has been one long out of body experience. I'm doing the things I always do, I know, making breakfast, going to work, doing the laundry, watching television, and whatever, and yet even as I'm doing these things, I feel like I have been watching myself do them from afar.

It reminds me of one of those late nights after a long day on the road, where I find myself in that driving zone. At first I'm just plugging along, listening to the radio, counting the miles, but then something changes, I begin to detach, and then it's as if I'm looking down from somewhere up above and watching myself at the wheel as I weave between the lights in front of me. There's no doubt that it's me that's driving and yet somehow I'm watching myself do it.

And that's where I'm at today, detached, and feeling kind of negative really. I told myself, and Kerri, for that matter, that today would be the only day that I would allow myself to think negative thoughts and that tomorrow I would get positive again, which I hope is true because those negative thoughts are creeping in.

It's like once I allow myself to think about the possibility of his death all sorts of roads open up. Take my children, my fathers' grandchildren, I don't have any yet, but will he never get to meet them when I do? And if so, will I tell them about him? And if I do, and I'll have to, what will I say? And where do I start? Or my mom, what happens to her? She says she will go on, but what does that mean? Will she continue to live at home? And if so will she live by herself? And go to work only to return to her empty house?

I also can't stop thinking about that scene in *Boyz In The Hood* when Ice Cube talks about the newspapers ignoring the death of his brother, like he's not important enough or something for the papers to talk about him. Will my dad go like that, with no one but us knowing or caring? And is that right?

He told me today that it isn't his time yet, that he has things to do. I know that, and want to believe it, but this is bad, and who knows what's going to happen.

Also, let's be honest, I can do other things, go to work, go for a run or watch the Knicks, but this is all I think about. In fact, I can't even remember a time when this wasn't our reality, and this despite the fact that we've only been in this place for a week or so.

It reminds me of the HIV+ folks from the support group I once co-lead and how they would say that there would be moments when they forgot about the fact that they were ill, maybe when they first awoke in the morning or when they got caught up in something at work. During those moments things felt normal again, but then they would let their guard down and it would all come back. And that's me, I will forget briefly as something catches my attention, but then just like that it's back, the fear, the sadness and the confusion.

I will get positive again though and this despite the problems we've had getting blood samples across the Mexican border where my Uncle Joe lives; and Fed Ex deliveries from way up in Maine on the lake where my uncle Larry lives; and despite the percentages; and his age; the disease's progression and the realities.

I will re-focus tomorrow. I will get positive and then maybe some good stuff will emerge. Maybe my parents will come out to Chicago for treatment regardless of which sibling my dad matches with. And maybe someday we will look back on this and laugh because it will have felt like one big out of body experience, like we were just watching something that never really happened, or at least happened such a long time ago it's hard to believe it was ever real.

4.

It is late and I know that I won't sleep. I will lie here. I will stare at the ceiling. I will masturbate, or if Kerri takes pity on me, we make love until the sheets are in tangles and covered with sweat and whatever fluids are left behind.

I will drink some water. I will go the bathroom. I will read The Nation, The New Yorker or Entertainment Weekly. I will smoke a joint and eat a container of Ben & Jerry's Cherry Garcia. I will watch several back-to-back episodes of ESPNews and then randomly channel surf hoping that *The Warriors*, *The Godfather* or *The Breakfast Club* will somehow randomly appear.

And then after all that and a million other things I do when I cannot sleep I will put on my running shoes and head out into the night, rolling into the park, past the statue of Lincoln in all of his glory, the softball fields, the lagoon, the harbors and totem poles.

At first and as always my breath will be labored and there will be kinks I need to work out. Muscles will be sore and knees tweaky. But slowly it will all fade away, the aches, the hurt, the loss and fear.

Somewhere out there in the night I will look back on a similar night many years before, back when the clutches of insomnia wrapped itself around my adolescent brain on a nightly basis and not just intermittently like it does now.

My parents would have been talking, talking, talking like they always did then, over coffee, and with Bruce

Springsteen singing somewhere in the background, and I had this sudden urge to put on my running shoes, something at the time I only did if I had track practice, and I went out into the night, gliding down the street to the track, my temple then, and I ran lap after lap, alone in the dark, the errant car passing by on the highway behind me, until I was stumbling and then half-jogging, half-hobbling back up the hill towards home, exhilarated, all powerful and floating just above the street.

When I walked into the house my parents looked at me, both confused and bemused, they hadn't seen me leave, and they could not believe I had been out running. They were speechless for the first time all night and following a brief wave I drifted off to bed, and then sleep, sweaty and triumphant.

5.

I go see my therapist. We've never really talked much about my dad, which is funny I suppose, though I almost never bring him up, so maybe it's not.

The therapist is what you might expect, or at least a version of what you might expect, with her curly black hair and slight, indistinguishable European accent, that I'm guessing might actually be Israeli.

She likes to wear turtleneck sweaters in soft, pastel colors, blues, greens and yellows. She speaks softly as well, gently. And she has these tiny hands that I try to not stare at during my sessions, but do so anyway, alternately freaked-out and turned on them by them. She doesn't push much, which I like, and probably ensures that I will keep coming back.

"How are you today," she says.

I decide to tell her about my father.

"I want to talk about my father," I say, "he's sick."

"Okay," she says, "go ahead"

"My father and I wrestled, fought really, all through my childhood, and into high school and then even when I got into college. And while these were battles full of headlocks and kidney punches and name calling, they weren't about anger or anything like that, nor were they even about winning. It was purely a tough guy thing, who was stronger, buffer, meaner and ultimately tougher. It's funny because my dad never held back or anything like that when I was little. He always went for the kill."

"Really, say more," the therapist says.

"He used to tell me this story about how one time when I was a little kid I put on my cape and grabbed these plastic swords I had and challenged him to a duel for my mom.

'So I challenged you to a duel,' I would say.

'Yeah, you put the cape on and came in with your swords and told me you wanted to fight.'

'Is that right, and I was like two years old maybe?'

'Yes, that seems right.'

'And you were down with that?'

'Sure I was.'

'And what happened next?'

'What do you mean what happened next,' he would always say, 'I kicked your ass.'

"Is that an important story for you?" the therapist asks.

"I suppose, I mean I think it captures all you need to know about him and us. And maybe that helps explain why I never held back much myself even as I grew bigger and stronger than my dad who was never such a big guy in the first place. He was like five foot eight or so and his forearms were all tensile from his years of working with his hands making art and writing. He was real skinny too, with this longish bird-like face, his dark eyes kind of small and almond shaped, his nose beakish, and his hair as wiry as his arms and fairly unkempt his entire adult life. And he was really tough, so I never fucked around regardless of how big I got and how old he got. We would generally square off like any two gladiators, circling each other warily, looking for the other to become distracted or off-balance and seeking an opportunity to strike. And this went on for years. Well, until the time my parents came to visit me this one weekend my sophomore year in college and we went to this fair that was out in this park off of college. The scene was just too perfect for a good fight, big open fields, soft grass, and lots of people milling around which allowed for a bit of an audience, and the question wasn't whether we would get into a fight, but when and why."

"And this was all in fun?" the therapist asks.

"Yes, totally, anyway, at some point we're out in this field and circling each other as we always did and then I got him onto his stomach and when he tried to get up onto the palm of his hands I yanked his right arm across his chest like I had probably done a hundred times before. This time though things went a little differently, because when I yanked his arm I heard this cracking sound. It was like a tree branch snapping. And we both immediately stopped what we were doing as did everyone in the area."

The therapist quietly gasps and brings her lovely, bird-like hands up to her mouth. I take a moment so I can stop staring at them and re-focus.

"I then hopped up and asked him whether he was okay. He got up, slowly, but under his own power. I could tell he was in pain, but he insisted everything was cool, gritting his teeth the whole time he was saying it, and still pretending he was fine even as we were separating some hours later and he couldn't raise his right arm above his waist as he tried to wave goodbye. A couple of days later my mom called and she told me that my dad had gone to open the car door that morning and when he had, his collarbone snapped. It had snapped, she said, because of the hairline fracture that had gone untreated since the weekend."

"How did that make you feel?" the therapist says.

"I don't know, but I don't think we ever wrestled again after that. It's funny though, talking about this now, and knowing that he's thinking about his life and the decisions he made, I wonder if anger on my part could have played a role in that accident."

"It could have," the therapist says.

"You know what else is funny though?" I ask.

"What?"

"I always thought my dad never held back when we fought, I even said it here today, but that must be impossible, how couldn't he have held back, I was so little."

"What does that mean to you?" she says.

"Huh, I guess it means that things aren't always what they seem to be and that you have to constantly revisit what you think you know, because it might all be wrong."

6.

I am at work. I work at a drop-in center for the homeless. When people first walk in, there is a ping pong table to their right and a bunch of couches to the left crowded around a television. After that there is a desk where we greet people and I am sitting at that desk, trying to greet people as they come in for lunch and trying my best to answer their questions.

Larry walks up and stares at me for a moment. Larry is probably my age. He lives in Lincoln Park, the actual park, not the neighborhood, and he says he has everything he needs there. We're just happy when he comes in at all.

"Hey man," Larry says, "I have this rash. I mean I think it's a rash. Could you take a look at it?"

"No man, I'd rather not," I say, "could you maybe talk to Janet, the nurse? She would probably be more helpful."

"Come on, I would really rather you look it," Larry says, "I trust you."

"All right, where is it?"

"It's right here," he says, "on the lower part of my butt, let me drop my pants."

"Oh, Larry no, please don't, not here at the desk."

He does anyway. It's definitely a rash.

Rhoda another client walks up and sits down next to me. She has big hair and big glasses and lives in the Catholic Workers House around the corner.

"Hello Rhoda," I say, "you need anything?"

"Nope, just hanging out, I like to be near you."

"That's nice, how are you doing?"

"Okay," she says.

"Good, are you taking your meds?"

"Nope, I feel like a zombie when I take them. I can't function that way."

"Yeah, but don't they help with the other stuff? The mania and the confusion, don't you feel more lucid and together?"

"Being lucid is overrated."

I can't disagree with that, though I suppose it is my job to do so. Rhoda gets real quiet after that and we just sit there until her boyfriend Jesse walks up. Jesse stares at Rhoda for a moment, never once looking at me.

"Let's go Rhoda, enough fraternizing," he says.

And then they're gone.

7.

Kerri and I are lying in bed. She's reading *Bastard out of Carolina* and I am reading the newspaper.

"Hey," I say.

"One second," she says not even looking at me, "this is really intense."

I wait one second.

"Hey," I say.

"One second, please," she says, "what are you, two-years old?"

"I haven't cried at all."

"Yeah," she says putting the book down and looking at me, "I noticed that, but then again, you never have cried much."

Which is true, I never liked crying, and I always thought I was above feeling anything that strongly, but I've changed, haven't I. You should have seen me at the end of the movie *Affliction*, I cried so hard I couldn't breathe. And yet, the tears don't come. Not when my heart feels heavy, nor, when I find myself pursing my lips or when my eyes start to brim with tears while looking at some dumb greeting card or just contemplating the what-ifs.

It might be denial of course. I am clearly not allowing myself to deal with this. Or it could be the surreal nature of this whole thing. I mean what exactly is going on? How did it happen? When did it happen? I don't care what the facts are.

In fact, I thought we all had this tacit agreement about how our little piece of the universe was going to work. We would go to family weddings and shoot pool and talk on the phone and fight at times, but it would all kind of make sense, there were rules and parameters that dictated our day-to-day existence. But now that's all been thrown out the window, nothing makes sense and the old rules no longer apply. That alone should be reason enough to cry though, shouldn't it?

"Hey," Kerri says lightly slapping me on the cheek, "you still there?"

"Yeah," I say rolling towards her, "sorry, I got lost in my thought there for a moment."

"You know," Kerri says smiling, her long, auburn hair falling across her face and pillow, "maybe this has something to do with the fact, that for a guy who never cried, and now pretty much only cries at movies, you're scared that if you let those tears come even a little, they're not ever going to stop coming?"

And this is a real possibility of course, because say I was to allow myself to cry, then what? How do I go on when all I want to do is cry, and when all I can do is focus on the horror of the whole thing?

I don't know. I haven't been there. I have no previous experience with this or any context to draw on. It's all new, all scary, and too horrible to even try to understand, much less open myself up to.

8.

Killing time, I never realized how terrible that phrase sounds when you use it at the wrong time, like when someone is actually dying. It sounds so completely wrong, and yet so many things do when you know someone who is dying.

If I don't eat something soon I just might starve to death, yes, death, I said it, I'm going to fucking die if I don't get a sandwich, like soon.

Really, I don't think so.

Still, I am killing time playing ping pong in the drop-in center. The bosses prefer that we don't play unless we are playing with an actual consumer, but everyone is smoking cigarettes, talking benefits with someone else or watching television, and so I am playing ping pong with my co-worker Marcus, who is a pretty intimidating dude. He is a six foot something black guy, with huge shoulders, a bald head and a fierce goatee. He was also a consumer himself once, homeless, drugs, all of it.

Marcus is winning 7-0. He always wins and he loves it.

"I am about to serve," he says, "and I'm going to your right with just a little backspin, so please try to prepare for it."

He serves and the ball whistles past me.

"What's up man," he says getting ready to serve again, "you always suck, but you really suck today, and while I am embarrassed for you, I'm always embarrassed for you, I'm also a little concerned, not a lot mind you, but enough to ask anyway."

Another serve whistles by me.

"What, are you trying to distract me with your fake empathy?" I say. "Nice."

"I said I was concerned, I didn't say I was going to go easy on you," Marcus replies, "I'm not your dad."

I pause.

"Sorry man," he says, "that was fucked-up."

"That's all right," I say, "I am thinking about my dad. I realized that today I thought a little bit less about the fact that he is so sick which made me feel guilty."

"You know man," he says, "you can't be in it all the time. That shit will kill you if you let it."

And there you go.

"Ah, man," he says smiling nervously.

The thing is, I am already not writing about this experience in my journal everyday either, which I had intended to do even if it was selfish to think that I might.

On the one hand this is troubling, because of what it says about life going on even when we are in the middle of a potentially life altering event. On the other hand though it is also troubling because of what it says about me.

It would be one thing if I were trying to write copious journal entries because I wanted to ensure that I wasn't missing a thing, but since I also know that I someday hope to write about all of this, I feel guilty about that as well. It's like being a vulture or rubbernecking at an accident, the main difference being you don't just stop to observe the accident, but you take notes as well.

Marcus is staring at me, waiting, and wondering if he's offended me. He hasn't, but that doesn't mean I can't use that to my advantage. I serve the ping pong, low and hard and he's nowhere near ready as it blows by him.

"Nine to one bitch," I say smiling.

I am back to killing time.

9.

"Why do we still watch *Saturday Night Live*?" Kerri asks.

We are lying on the couch. We have been flipping channels. We might have sex. We might not. We might talk about my dad. We might not. We might move off of the couch at some point tonight. We might not. But we have decided to watch *Saturday Night Live*.

"It's not funny anymore is it?" Kerri says.

My father's favorite *Saturday Night Live* skit is one where a very elderly John Belushi goes to a cemetery and visits the graves of all his old co-stars. While there he ruminates on the fact that he has outlived them because he was a dancer.

He then proceeds to dance on their graves.

The show is not funny anymore, but I watch it because my dad liked to watch it. I watch it because we do things our parents did without even consciously knowing we are doing them. I watch it because my dad will likely be dead sooner than later and I need to hold onto whatever I have of him.

10.

"So what do you know about Thalidomide?" my dad says to me.

I lift myself up onto my elbows and look over at him. We are lying in bed in our hotel room, watching the British Open and trying to stay cool.

It's hot, so very hot, and because it's so hot everywhere you look there are dead people, dead crops and lots of dust, the most since the Dust Bowl according to the President. We also have unprecedented drought conditions in the mid-Atlantic, and lots of people praying for lots of rain.

The family is in Baton Rouge for Jerry's wedding and it is the kind of hot down here that the best man ought to have a handkerchief handy to wipe the groom's brow. But he didn't.

The British Open is interrupted for a news break. JFK Jr., his wife, and sister-in-law are missing, plane crash or something. It's all anyone can talk about. And there is a sense that while they may very well find the bodies, and that they might even still be alive, the chances seem slimmer and slimmer with each passing moment.

The whole thing feels like a tragedy, similar to Princess Diana's car crash, and yet on a very selfish level I resent all the attention the accident is receiving. I certainly don't wish death upon JFK Jr. and his family anymore than on anyone else, but I also don't know what he has done to deserve this outpouring of grief.

Of course, it has nothing to do with what he has done, but who he is. JFK, Jr. is a rock star. No, he's more than that, and he's more than a celebrity. Maybe he's even royalty. Well, no matter what he is, he will always be the little boy saluting his dead father. So yeah, I know why he's getting all of this attention, and maybe, maybe even why he's being called a hero, but it doesn't change the fact that my father who is likely to die sometime soon won't receive anything remotely similar.

Is JFK Jr. a bigger hero than my father? I don't know if either of them are heroes, but one of them has the dead father, and the assassinated uncle, and the endless family history of pain, and so somehow his loss is more tragic. The thing is, even as we lie here in our air-conditioned hotel room, trying to protect my dad from whatever horrible things lurk outside I just don't know what's going to happen or if it even matters.

"So what do you know about Thalidomide?" my dad says to me again as I realize that I was lost in thought there for a moment.

"Not much," I respond, "isn't it banned. It fucks up fetuses doesn't it?"

"Yes, that's right," he responds, "but as it turns out it might be a treatment option for me."

"Really, that seems weird, but you're not pregnant, so what's the difference, right? You're not pregnant are you?"

"No, baby, I'm not pregnant, nothing like that. Chemotherapy is also an option," he continues, "after that they can then do an autologous transplant."

"What's that?"

"It's the harvesting and transplantation of temporarily healthy bone marrow, and non-related, or non-familial, bone marrow transplants."

"Jesus, you almost sound smart," I say.

And then we both laugh.

What's fucked-up though, is that the only reason we are reading up on all this stuff is because we now know that there is no sibling match.

We stop laughing and my dad gets a serious look on his face.

"I really thought one of my brothers would be able to hook me up with some matching bone marrow after all I did for them as kids," he says. "What a kick in the head."

His brother Joe isn't a match, and Larry just doesn't want to donate. He took the test, and he mailed the blood, but he doesn't want to do it. I wonder what's wrong with people, and I wonder if given the chance, how many times I could kick Larry in the head before someone stopped me.

I don't dwell on this though, because here we are, and we have no match, and who knows what the fuck that means.

11.

The therapist really is sort of cute. Nice mouth. Jewish-looking. And those hands, those tiny hands I just want to eat like marzipan. I don't think I have anything to talk about today though. Maybe she will have some ideas.

"Do you have anything you would like to talk about today?" she asks.

I wonder if she would sleep with me. I'm not saying I want to, or would, but I am wondering.

"Not much," I reply.

"Nothing," she says.

"Eh."

"What about your dad, what's going on there?"

My dad. Right.

"I'm not sure which I find more amazing," I say, "that one of my dad's doctor's actually told him he might as well go home and enjoy the rest of his life because there isn't much anyone can do for him at this point or that no one, doctors, nurses, whomever, seems to have any idea what he should do now that he has been diagnosed. Shouldn't someone somewhere, some organization, or some something be able to talk to my father and our family about his options, and possible next steps, regardless of how bleak things may be? Why is that along with the incessant efforts of my parents it was ultimately Kerri that stumbled on a protocol being done at Johns Hopkins? And why is it that when my father approached his doctor and asked him if he thought entering this protocol might be a good idea, or whether he had even heard of the particular doctor leading it, his doctor said oh sure, doctor so and so at Hopkins, I refer people to her all the time."

The therapist starts to say something, but I'm on a roll now.

"Are patients completely responsible for taking the lead on this shit, and if so how Darwinian has medicine become? Are only the strongest of the weak expected to survive? Is that okay with the American public? It could drive you crazy if you let it, but then what, nobody would get the treatment they need. Of course maybe that's part of the plan. Isn't it easier, and cheaper, if people die off at home, alone, untreated, and out of the way?"

And then I stop.

"Let's talk about this," the therapist says.

12.

I'm sitting with my mom in my old room. She's crying and I am trying not to. I would love to be more supportive than I feel right now, because the fact is I don't really want anyone crying around me, ever. I can suck it up for my mom, but I don't want it, and especially from her, she was the real rock in the house when we were growing-up.

Meanwhile, what I want to do is talk to her, because after all the information about potential treatment options has been gathered and after all the questions about these options has been asked. After all the doctors have voiced their opinions, and even after I think I have decided on at least what I think the best treatment option is, chemotherapy at Johns Hopkins with hopes for a remission, albeit brief, so an autologous transplant can be attempted, I still have to wonder whether we have made the right decision.

The fact is I can go home for the weekend and I can help my father with all the chores he meant to do for so long, filing stories and articles, gathering random 8' by 10' photos, and we can muse about what could have been, or should have been.

I can even watch my father in his now frailer state, so skinny and weak all of a sudden, talking and moving certainly, but more slowly than ever before, take stock of his life and open himself up to memories and questions and what ifs.

But I still have to wonder what the right decision regarding treatment is and whether I can ever know for sure. I also have to wonder why him and why now? It isn't like he's as old as the other patients I see in the cancer ward, or has something as scary, but in comparison as benign, as prostate cancer.

"Mom, mom," I say.

"Yeah, honey," she says, wiping her eyes and focusing in me.

"Why did he get this disease? Can anyone explain this in any rational or irrational way?"

"I don't think we know sweetie."

"He's not going to talk about death or fear or anything like that," I say, "but he wants to know if it's because he wasn't religious enough or because he didn't move to Jerusalem. And I wonder about this too. Is it some sort of karma thing?"

"I don't know, I don't believe in that," she says, "but you need to believe in whatever helps."

"I know he was questionable as a husband at times, but never as a father. Well, not entirely."

"I don't want to talk about us," she says, "it was a long time ago, and we're good. And he was a great father. He loved you so much when you were born."

"So, what, is all this just an anomaly, unexplainable and statistically obtuse, not to mention obscene?"

"I don't know. We don't know."

And we don't. And he and I haven't really talked about it yet. What we have talked about though it is what is best for him, where he should go for treatment and what he should have done. It has been crazy and tense and discussed until it cannot be discussed any more. I have to remember to be patient as I talk about it with him though, because this is someone's, and not just anyone's, life we are talking about here.

Eventually everyone feels chemotherapy at Johns Hopkins is the way to go and when all is said and done, and as my mom and I sit on the couch in my old room, I am reminded of my childhood and the times my dad would leave. I never had any idea what to do or say then and I can't say I feel any different now.

13.

I go out. Kerri doesn't want a drink, but doesn't care that I do and so I'm gone. Off to Thirsty's for one Yuengling and then another. There are no plans for more than one drink, maybe two, but one becomes three, then five, and then there's some chick who says we went to high school together, and maybe we did.

She's leaning in to talk and touching my leg, and she has long brown hair and a big smile, and I know I shouldn't do this, but tonight I deserve to act out and not act like myself, just once, don't I? How could anyone call me on this?

I'm in pain. I've got a dying father and this girl has something to offer, something almost medicinal, and it's okay then, okay, okay, okay, something I keep telling myself as we have sex in the backseat of her car, legs everywhere, and then I walk back to my father's house, stopping long enough to shower once there before climbing into bed with Kerri and drifting off to sleep, drunk and restless.

14.

I am at work and I am walking to the office I share with Marcus, which is at the end of the hall, past the drop-in center, the nurse's office and the lunchroom where I and the other freaks endlessly map-out the black oil mythology of the *X-Files* on the whiteboard over the lunch table.

Standing by my door is Lola, a beautiful, cross-dressing male prostitute who makes rent, when he isn't spending his earnings on crystal meth, by trolling the hotel bars up and down Michigan Avenue and sucking-off business men who are otherwise happily married, but happen to be travelling for work.

Lola doesn't say anything, but after I dump my bag and walk back towards the bathroom he follows silently, just steps behind me. Lola continues to not say anything as I urinate and wash my hands. He just stands there staring at my back, his arms crossed on his chest and a small smile creeping across the thick layer of foundation caked onto his otherwise beautiful face.

Lola silently follows me down the hall, and when I get back to my door, he quickly darts in front of me and then stands there, facing me, still smiling, arms still crossed and not saying a word.

"Yes," I say, "what's up?"

Nothing. More smiling.

"Can I help you?" I ask.

"Do you want to fuck sometime," Lola says, "for you it will be free of charge."

"I'm sorry, but I'm married," I say, even as I wonder what it would be like to be blown by Lola in the park across from The Drake.

"You're married, so what," Lola says, "do you know how many married guys I do? What does that matter?"

What does it matter I wonder, even as Trina, a hulking crack head, starts screaming at someone down the hall, which distracts Lola long enough to allow me to make my escape before I have to come up with a reasonable answer to that question.

15.

Things are happening, and they're crazy, and it's hard to get a handle on any of it. And no, I don't mean the ransacking of East Timor or the Middle East Final Status talks. Nor am I talking about Venezuela's Democratic tumble or George W. Bush's continued moneyed rise to the top, even though all of these things are being reported on by CNN, which endlessly plays on the television across the room from my father's hospital bed as he fitfully naps throughout the day.

No, what I'm actually talking about is how I have just flown to Baltimore and Johns Hopkins for the second time in three weeks and how every moment when I stop to pause and think and catch my breath I tend to focus on one thing, the craziness enveloping my family, and more specifically my father.

His blood counts while fluctuating are climbing, and that's good, but even if they continue to climb, what if they aren't healthy? Or what if they are, will the autologous transplant be successful? And what if it is? That might mean two years or more, but then is that it? Or, does he then roll into an unrelated match? And will he even find an unrelated match? It's like a one out of four million chance.

It's all so confusing and somewhat deceiving, self-deceiving anyway, being here with him. Because aside from the thinning hair and the need for all of us to constantly wash our heads and avoid kissing him on the lips, he looks a lot better then he has been looking, almost normal really. His energy seems up. His fatigue somewhat lessened.

I want to believe that means something and maybe it does, especially when he wakes up in the hospital and looks happy to see me. But then as he looks up at the television, he gets nostalgic as we listen to a news report about the Outer Banks in North Carolina because it takes him back to a long ago family trip, and a beat-up ferry that had a hot dog stand. And the memory makes him sad, and the tears start to well-up, first for him, and then for me, and then it's not so deceiving. Reality hits and I have to ask, or at least wonder, how long do we really have, because it can't be too much longer.

16.

My dad was nostalgic yesterday at Johns Hopkins and today it's my turn as I sit here at the therapist's office trying to avoid staring at her hands and be in the moment.

"My dad has always worn the cheapest brown leather work boots he could find," I tell her. "He never owned any other type of shoe, and he wore every pair of boots he ever bought into the ground. This idea of wearing things until they disintegrated is important because it was his general philosophy when it came to wardrobe. He also wore the same brown leather belt for as long as I can remember and rarely strayed from the same basic uniform that he wore much of his adult life, the shoes, the belt, whatever beat-up jeans he was wearing at that time, and a white or blue oxford shirt passed down from my brother or I and or some t-shirt my parents brought back from a trip they had gone on that we had refused to wear and he had retained. My father in fact bragged that he rarely had to buy clothes because he could always count on us to pass things along to him."

"How did that make you feel" the therapist asks, her hands like little birds building a nest in her lap.

"How did that make me feel, what do you mean?"

"His style was unusual, unorthodox, and that might have been difficult as an adolescent who just wants to fit in."

"Oh," I say, "I got you. You know, I was once asked whether I was embarrassed about his sense of style. What

I said, is that I never really was, because on the one hand I recognized that people thought he was fairly cool, and on the other there was the *Hotel New Hampshire* by John Irving."

"The book?"

"Yeah, when I was a kid I read the *Hotel New Hampshire* and there is a section of the book where the remaining family is living in Vienna and the narrator goes out for drinks with his father to this fancy bar. The son is concerned about being seen with the father who is quite eccentric in dress and personality. When they get inside the bar though it turns out that the father is a regular there and the patrons all love him for who he is regardless, or maybe because, of how he dresses and what that represents to them."

"So, it wasn't a problem then?"

"No, that was the least of the problems."

17.

All hail Southwest Airlines. They love to celebrate the fact that their flights are always on time, and yet both of the flights I had to catch today have been late. Of course, if I weren't angry about the flights and the hassle I would probably be looking for something, or someone, to be angry at.

My grandmother, my father's mother, has died, and even though it's unbelievably fucked up that we had to lose her at all, much less right now, here I am with Kerri jetting off to New York by way of Baltimore so everyone can convene at the Schwartz Funeral Home in Queens. Having to make the connecting flight in Baltimore is not as annoying as it might normally be, however, because it has given me the chance to meet my parents at the airport and fly with them to New York.

There had been a real question about whether the doctors at Hopkins were going to let my dad out of the hospital for the funeral, but they did, and there he is. It's amazing just how tired, older and sicker he looks in his heavy sweater, coat, baseball cap and mask. Also, note to self, never make fun of people in masks again. Not even in my head. Not even if it's Michael Jackson.

Anyway, we come down the hall at the airport and we see my parents, looking like they always look, but not exactly. My dad is kind of shuffling, half his face covered by the mask that just yells sick guy to the world, and the other half covered by the bill of his baseball cap. His skin color is off too, ashy, and he looks so tired I am half tempted to throw him over my shoulder and carry him onto the plane.

But then we learn that we can board the plane early because of his condition, something that seems really cool until we see how empty the plane actually is.

We take our seats and any further thoughts on the intricacies of Southwest's boarding policies are quickly lost first to conversation about my dad's health and then to my feelings about the guy sitting in the row behind my parents who complains to us that we are talking to loudly.

"My father is dying of cancer," I scream. "He's been in the hospital receiving chemo for weeks and he was only released early so he can attend his mother's funeral. Now, I will assume you didn't know this, but now that you do, would it be asking too much for you to shut the fuck-up, you overly primped, dumb-ass, Coogi sweater wearing North shore motherfucker?"

The guy looks at me and at first he is taken aback, but then apparently feeling like he has to be tough, he says, "I'm not scared of you, you little punk, fuck-off."

I could be cool here and recognize that this guy may in fact be an overly primped, dumb-ass, Coogi sweater wearing North shore motherfucker, but that doesn't mean I shouldn't rise above my anger and be the bigger, and better, person.

Instead, however, I climb over the two rows of seats between us, and staring into his now incredulous face I tell him that he can keep his opinion to himself or he can fucking move to one of the many open seats behind him.

I want him to respond poorly. Instead, he pauses. He weighs his options. And then he just stares at me, not speaking, just waiting. Waiting to see what I will do and smiling just a bit, the corners of his mouth crinkling ever so slightly. Maybe he thinks this will defuse the moment. Or maybe he thinks I don't have the balls to do something. Regardless, this drives me nuts.

I punch him in his stupid face and then not being able to hold back I punch him again and again until I can't see his stupid face anymore.

Well, this is how I want it all to go down. In reality though, I do not say a word to him, or climb over any seats, or even punch him. Instead I just sit there, stewing in my anger the rest of the flight, feelings of powerlessness firmly intact.

18.

We are sitting around the bed in a crappy hotel room near the cemetery. The rug is ripped and moist. The furniture is old and chipped. The air is muggy and thick. My dad needs to take his medicine and as my mom goes to get it I stretch out on the bed and close my eyes.

My grandmother went in her sleep and most would have you believe that this was a good thing because it was seemingly painless and peaceful. I hope that's true. They would also have you believe that after all her suffering the last couple of years, everything from Emphysema to broken hips, that she has gone on to a better place. I of course hope that's true as well, but either way, she's gone and I'm sad, sad certainly for selfish reasons, but also because she spent so much of her time angry, bitter and disappointed, and it pains me that anyone, particularly my grandmother should have had to live out their final years like that.

And yet, despite all of this, it pains me even more that my father in his sickened and tortured state has to wade through the feelings, emotions and conflict that come with her passing. He too is disappointed, bitter and angry in many ways, and while these emotions do not remotely reflect who or what he is, her death is one more area where no closure will be available to him as he takes stock of his life.

On top of all that the news continues to be poor for him. There will be no autologous transplant because there has been no remission. Another option has been snuffed and so we will try to look forward and we will try to believe and hope that there are still possibilities and that not all is lost.

Of course then I open my eyes and remember where I am, laying with him in his crappy hotel bed and hoping to comfort him like he used to do for me so many years ago. He's drained, his hair is wispy and he's getting his antibiotics through the IV line that he and my mother have somehow set-up. I look at him in this new place and I have to wonder whether there really is hope, because wanting it to be doesn't make it so. I don't care what anyone tells me.

19.

The funeral is over, my dad is back home and after briefly going back to Chicago I am back home now as well, in the house I grew-up in, sitting on the floor, talking, reading, and waiting, waiting for the beep that is soon to come. The beep warns my father that he is out of antibiotics. He knows this, and it is okay, except that he doesn't know how to shut off the computer that controls the flow of the antibiotics and he can't get more antibiotics until his home health-aid arrives an hour or more from now. There is a silence button though, not unlike the snooze button on an alarm clock, and my job is to press that button every time I hear the beep so he can try to get some sleep.

Which is why I am sitting here in the semi-darkness as the light creeps through the shades and the dust dances before me every time it hits a shard of light. I am pressing the silence button, and I keep pressing the button, even as his breath deepens, and even as he emits intermittent moans. I sit here staring at the dust and I think about just how crazy this all still seems, how I got here and what's going to happen.

The fact is, I can press buttons forever, and I can sit guard over my father, but that doesn't mean I can control anything and there's no reason to pretend I can. This week he was not only struck with pneumonia and watched his temperature spike to 105 degrees, but he found out that an unrelated donor he had matched with was willing to donate, but not medically able to do so.

And so it goes. Or doesn't. No breaks, no luck, and no news, but the bad kind. So I sit by his bed, bewildered and befuddled, pressing the silence button, still wanting to be hopeful, but wondering if whether like Kafka's hunger artist he will be a little weaker and thinner each visit until that thing happens, that thing I can't say out loud, at least not too loudly, not yet anyway.

20.

Kerri and I are in bed, naked and eating Haggen-Dazs ice cream. Why can't every night be like this?

"What are you thinking about?" she asks.

"You have to ask?"

"Stop, besides that," she says smiling before turning her head towards me. "Are you thinking about anything else? And please say you are."

"I guess, can I tell you a story?"

"Of course."

"All right, so there was this time when I was twelve years old and my dad asked me if I wanted to shoot pool with him. I have to admit now that I wasn't really into playing back then because I found the game to be endlessly frustrating. I would try to line up shots, but the cue ball never went where it was supposed to go, the balls flew all over, I was constantly scratching and it just didn't seem worthwhile. Still, shooting pool had been his thing as a kid and that alone held great allure for me. When I added in the fact that he just wasn't always living home then and wanted to go shoot at the arcade where the cool high school kids hung out it was impossible to pass on. Anyway, we go to the arcade, and the room was real smoky and there were arcade games everywhere, Centipede and Pole Position and Asteroids and Pac Man…"

"I loved Centipede," Kerri says pulling the blanket over her nakedness.

"I know, I listen," I say.

"Sure you do," she says.

"Sometimes I do," I say, "so, lights were flashing, bells were ringing and the room was filled with surly, long-haired, teenagers, wearing wispy mustaches, both the boys and the girls, and baseball-style concert t-shirts emblazoned with Iron Maiden iconography and tour dates. I felt like I had invaded some sort of hidden teenage sanctum and it was all a bit scary really. In fact, I would have been just as happy to leave, but I certainly wasn't going to say anything to my dad, who seemed really comfortable there. These were his people though, surly, blue collar outsiders, who just happened to be teenagers, which like him, made them all think they were way tougher than they were. I could have left at any moment, but soon realized there was no turning back when he placed his two quarters on the side of table for winners."

Kerri shifts positions, throwing her leg over mine, her bare stomach on my hip. I stop for a moment and stroke her leg. I enjoy the moment, the silence, the skin, the sheer naked connectedness of the moment. And then I continue with my story.

"So, we stood there until the game being played was over, I nervous that we might actually have to play, my dad all calm, even Zen. And then the winners looked over at us and my dad racked. The teenagers broke. They were okay and I missed every shot, but my dad was awesome, using English, hitting shots from every possible angle, and never talking, just cruising around the table like Fast Eddy Felson and doing his thing. Soon enough the game was over, we were the winners and just like that we owned the table."

I look over and Kerri is dozing, eyes mostly open, but not exactly.

"I'm up," she says suddenly bursting forward.

"Sure you are," I say.

"I am," she says, "pool, teenagers, got it."

"Right, so the next set of teenagers approach the table.

They racked, and we broke, and I didn't hit a fucking thing, but it didn't matter, because there was my dad once again walking around that table in his ratty jeans and old oxford stalking those balls, not missing a shot. He was a god out there."

"Yeah."

"Yeah, and then just like that we won again. At this point the whole place is watching, but they had to, who were we to come into their space and take over? And who was this old guy running every shot? No one could answer those questions and no one immediately emerged to challenge us for the table either. Instead the teenagers conferred amongst themselves and then decided to send their two best players, two chicks with brunette Farrah do's, to challenge us."

"I loved the Farrah do too," Kerri says eyes closed.

"I know that as well, I listen, really," I say. "So, anyway, the girls could really play, and no, they weren't better then my dad, but he'd been carrying me up until that point. Soon they were going ball for ball with us and the place is totally silent, everyone watching, not talking, just staring, the four of us in our own little world. With each dropped ball the tension mounted, and then there is just the eight ball. The one girl misses it, leaving it just sitting there by the pocket waiting for someone to knock it in."

"It's like Hoosiers."

"Yes, sure, except for the drunken dad thing, but yes, and it's my shot. It's a lot of green, and the girls are already getting ready for their next shot because they know I'm going to miss it. The thing is, it's a straight enough shot, and my dad is coaching me, and so I line it up. The room at this point is collectively holding its breath. They want me to miss the shot. They need me to miss it."

"But you wouldn't do that would you?" Kerri says curling into fetal position.

"We'll see. I tap the cue ball. A slight waft of chalk curls up above the table and contorts in the lights. The cue ball makes its long journey across the table, meandering a bit where the table is warped, and hopping when it encounters cigarette burns. It stays true to the line though and even as it begins to lose what little momentum it has, it kisses the eight ball dead center. The world stops revolving for just a moment, and as if we needed any more drama, the eight ball briefly rolls back and forth on the lip of the pocket before dropping safely into the scarred leather net below. We are triumphant. The room is dejected. And we leave as undefeated, never once beat, in your face champions. My father and I didn't shoot much stick after that until many years later, but he would tell that story over and over again, the day I, all calm, cool, and collected hit the shot that beat the girls. Cool, right?"

No response. Kerri is unconscious and lost to the night.

21.

There has been some discussion at work about whether we should talk to Trina about attending rehab because there is a bed that has just become available. She has not received this suggestion well in the past though. She does not feel she has a problem with crack. A problem she has explained to anyone who will listen implies that she has no control over the situation. Or that she cannot stop any time she wants. But she does have control she says and she can stop anytime she wants. She just doesn't want to.

We decide that Marcus should discuss this with her. Marcus lived on the streets. Marcus smoked crack for many years. Marcus sort of knew her then. And Marcus is a big dude and physically imposing, which we think will help the situation, because Trina is also physically imposing, and high, never a great combination.

After Marcus informs Trina that the bed is available, she responds much as we anticipated. She squares her shoulders and starts jabbing her finger in his face, leaning in as close to Marcus as she can.

"I don't have a problem motherfucker," she says. "You have the problem. Maybe what I need to do is get my knife and stab you in the fucking eye? Better yet, maybe I need to surprise you in an alley, or on the "L" tracks, or at your home. Yes, I know where you live motherfucker, and maybe I should stab you there right in front of your new family and that new baby. How does that sound motherfucker?"

Marcus never moves, not one step, not one muscle, he just lets her spew until she runs out of steam. He is calm and he is amazing, never taking the bait, never becoming confrontational. I know there is a lesson here about how to comport oneself under stress and how to face what one fears headfirst, always staying as calm as possible, betraying nothing. I hope to be that calm someday if the situation calls for it. I also hope I never have to find out if I can be.

Trina soon walks away and Marcus walks away shortly after she does and since he doesn't come back, I don't get to speak to him until the next day.

"Dude, you were amazing yesterday," I say. "Textbook, how did you do that? What's the secret?"

"I don't know for sure, "Marcus says, "but what I do know is that after I left the office, I walked all the way home and ate an entire Entenmann's cake in one sitting."

22.

My parents have come to Chicago. They have come to learn about Thalidomide. And like so many other doctors pushing their research the doctor here has tried to sell them on the wondrous possibilities of this once banned drug.

"It's a miracle drug. We're saving lives. We'll save your life, or at least extend it. You sound like such a great candidate. You must come, and you must come at once, for a consultation."

And so they do.

The doctor didn't mention, however, how few people they have really treated or how few people they have really saved. A fifty percent success rate is spectacular, but is it spectacular when you have only treated four people and two have survived longer than expected? The doctor didn't ask about my dad's age over the phone either. Or how far advanced my father's case might be. But she does when my parents arrive for their appointment. My dad looks old, and sick and tired, and because of this the doctor is not so positive when they arrive, not dismissive, but different, not as enthused or as flirtatious as she had been on the phone. I know she's wondering whether he's going to help her research or fuck up the numbers, because there cannot be any bad candidates when funding is riding on this.

So then there we are, all of us, nowhere exactly, but together anyway and trying to decide what to do to avoid thinking about the appointment, the latest disappointment on the long road to nowhere we are currently traversing.

My dad asks whether I want to shoot some pool. I'm not sure that he can stand long enough to do so, but as I have been wondering whether the two of us would ever play again I jump at the opportunity.

We go to Dave and Busters, which is cheesy for sure, but it has nice tables, and more importantly it is close by, which is crucial.

"If you want to know the truth," I tell him, "I feel kind of guilty taking advantage of a sick guy."

"Well, that's alright, take your time."

"Cool, fasten your seatbelt then."

"Hey, how's work," he asks just as I'm lining up my shot and just in time to distract me.

"Its fine," I say, all the time worrying about whether he's comfortable enough and whether or not he's going to topple over.

"Are you writing at all?" I ask.

"No," he says, "I can't do it."

"Can't, or won't?" I ask.

"I can't bear to leave any more unpublished work lying around," he says.

"But you don't know it will go unpublished," I say, "you never really know, do you?"

"Hey, see that shot," he says, after tapping one in and completely ignoring my comment.

"Are you doing any drawing?" I ask. "Maybe it would help?"

"Maybe, hey, you see that shit," he says tapping in another ball and then sitting down to catch his breath.

"Not bad, not bad for a really sick motherfucker like you," I say, "how are you feeling?"

"Good, alright, well, maybe kind of tired. Maybe we should stop soon."

Which we do, which means we're done almost as soon as we have started, which is nothing like the old days when we might play for hours, swigging coffee and talking shit.

But these are not the old days and when all is said and done, maybe it's not hopeful or anything. In fact, maybe it's even kind of painful to watch the whole thing, but it is something good in the midst of a whole lot of bad, and we will take any of that we can find.

23.

Long after we are done playing pool, I am lying in bed next to Kerri and listening to her breath. My head is spinning and I cannot fall asleep. I want her to wake-up, but she is not doing so on her own. I try and will her to wake-up instead, intensely concentrating on her eyes opening, her rolling over and looking at me.

I also picture us fooling around, though that is just a bonus.

Nothing is happening. Apparently my superhero powers aren't as strong as I thought. I cough, nothing, I kiss her on the cheek, still nothing. I spoon her and run my fingers through her hair. She arches her back into my stomach and stops breathing for a moment. This is hopeful, but then the breathing resumes. I decide to just wake her.

"Honey, Kerri? Are you awake?"

No. I push her shoulder. Just a little and she rolls over.

"What, what the fuck dude," she says, her eyes still closed, "someone better be fucking dying."

I laugh, despite how fucked-up that is.

"Someone is," I respond.

"Yeah, right, okay, I'm sorry," she says groggily, "kind of sorry, what's up?"

"I was thinking about time," I say.

"Okay," she says, "what does that mean?"

"My father was given a year to a year and a half to live if not treated successfully, right?" I ask.

"Right."

"And if a sibling match was successful, he would have had five years at the minimum, though without one he could have maybe three to six months."

"Uh-huh."

"If he gets an autologous transplant, which is no curative, the doctors are seeing people living for upwards to two years if they can get one. He would be living in a weakened state and he would need a remission first, which is only good for about a month, but that could be two more years and who knows what they'll discover between now and then."

"Also, correct."

"Then there was that non-related match, but that guy is off the donor base for three months because he isn't medically viable, and now, given my father's current condition, and with his counts as they are, he probably only has a month before the doctors will recommend another chemo regime because he really can't wait any longer for the other not so great match that has possibly emerged."

"Baby you're bugging out here," Kerri says, "why are we running through all of this, and so late at night, what's up?"

"It's just that with each new announcement it's a whole new window or time frame for him and for us and guess I cannot figure out what I should be doing to maximize that time? How often should I visit? How many calls should I make to him between visits? What questions should I ask him? Are there things I want to know? Are there things he wants to tell me? How much or how little is right or enough? How much more can I do? There is the time I have and the time I don't and I just don't know how much of either is available to me."

"Enough," Kerri says. "You're totally spinning. Just come here okay."

Kerri starts stroking my hair and I slowly start to calm down. Soon I am actually feeling tired and trying to keep my eyes open, but I can't. I see Marcus and I'm not sure what he's doing in the apartment or where Kerri went. Marcus tells me that he found my dad floating in the building's pool. I immediately assume he has drowned, though I know he has died because his illness has caught up with him, like we know, for better or worse, and in the long term or short, will happen now. I stand by the pool looking at him, floating there in his jeans and a blue oxford, and I begin to sob uncontrollably, at first because he is dead and then because I recognize that I am having a dream and I wonder if the dream means that he has died while I slept. I continue to sob as I awake, the first time since the diagnosis. I realize that he will die sooner or later as we all do, but much sooner then we all expected. It's a time thing and its presence looms larger than life these days.

24.

Ah, Thanksgiving, hope flows, ebbs and flows again. My dad and I are standing out on the back porch. The sky is gray, with streaks of orange and pink. The trees looming over us are lush, a mix of purples and reds, it is fall in upstate New York, a multi-colored world of thanks and joy overshadowed by the chill in the air and the sense that not only winter awaits, but all the metaphors therein.

My dad is grilling the turkey and not talking, though for no particular reason I know of. Still, I have not been willing, or able, to initiate conversation of any kind and this apparently is fine with him.

There was yet another possible donor and a mini-transplant regime being discussed at the Fred Hutchinson Center in Seattle. For a moment, a brief moment, there even seemed to be a variety of options to choose from, and right here, and right now, my dad seems so strong, and so it's nice to wonder if we are in fact turning some sort of corner, even when just recently there seemed to be no corners to turn.

I want to believe, not just be hopeful and positive and supportive, but believe, but can I, really? Because as it turns out there was ultimately no donor, nor any mini-transplant regime, there was the belief they existed, but ultimately there is just the Thalidomode option in Chicago, which might not be so bad, if it were not so unproven and so much was unknown.

He does seem strong though and so I try to believe, the thing is I just wish, that either way, maybe, just maybe, he could stop obsessing about so much about every little detail of every possible treatment, and his insurance coverage, and who knows what. Because it has to be torturous and isn't he tortured enough? He's dying and doesn't even know why. He's lost his mother. And he has to think about the wrongs he feels he inflicted on our family. There's also the work, and the success he wanted, but never quite got, and who knows what else is running through his head.

And while I don't know what's running through his head, I have to believe that one thing he's thinking about is death, but I don't know if this is the case, because we're not talking and I'm not asking. I imagine I could ask, but what then? He never broaches the possibility that he is, or at least might be, dying, and so neither do I. The question of course is whether I do not ask for his sake or mine?

"Hey dad," I say, "what are you thinking about?"

"Nothing much, just wondering if this grill is hot enough, whether the turkey is cooking and how it is you ever really know for sure if you know what you're doing despite how many times you've done it before."

"I'm not sure if we're still talking turkey here, no pun intended…"

"Of course not."

"…but there is a lot going on, is there anything you want to talk about?"

"Actually with your being home, I was thinking about Jessie."

"Jessie?"

"Yeah, you know, the girl from the lawn."

25.

Jessie. The sign above the clock in math class read, "Time will pass, will you?" It is a very legitimate question most days and one I had spent many nights fretting over. Today though, dividing fractions and failing grades were not enough to draw my attention away from the clock. I counted each passing second waiting desperately for the school day to end so I could make my escape. And when the bell finally rang I tore out of my seat each moment taking one step closer to freedom. Or so I thought.

At first I didn't see her. We weren't in the same math class and so I figured I could make my move before she even realized I was out of the building. But then out of the corner of my eye I spotted her, and before I could slip into the crowd she spotted me too. It was at this point that I knew I was dead in my tracks.

At first she had just stared at me in class. Soon though, she had started trying to get on line next to me during lunch, asking for "frontsies" and that kind of thing. Then she started following me home, at first once a week maybe and then almost every day. She had never come all the way to the house, but she was inching closer every time and I knew it was not a question of if at this point, but when.

And then when arrived, and it was today, and as I left the building she was right there behind me, shadowing my every step, silent and focused. She followed me to the cross walk, fought past the crossing guard and proceeded to head up the street towards my house.

It evidently mattered little to her that her love, nay her obsession was unrequited. She wanted me in the way only a fifth grade girl truly can. And so what if I walked away from her whenever she approached, and who cared that I wouldn't respond to her love notes or lip sync "Summer Loving" with her at the talent show. She had to be near me. She had to possess me. And that of course was where the dread truly came from. It didn't matter what I did or did not do, for there was no escape.

On this day though, I did not have the time to weigh these thoughts or their ramifications at any great length, because on this day she just would not stop following me, and there truly was no escaping her. Soon I just stopped looking back, hoping somehow that if I didn't pay attention to her she would just go away. But she didn't go away, or, couldn't I guess. She had invested too much now and there was no turning back.

I kept pretty cool until I saw the house, but then the panic set in, and the sweat began to trickle down my back and my stomach began to knot up. Soon I was running like never before, my canvas Nikes slapping the pavement, only one goal in mind, reaching the front door untouched and unscathed. As the door closed behind me, I knew I had made it, and it was triumphant.

I knew that tomorrow would surely bring more such terror, but once safely inside I lay back on the couch to soak up the moment, savor my victory, and rest up for the nightly neighborhood stickball game. It was all quite glorious really, and short-lived, because moments later my father walked in, this being the 1970's version, crazy hair, bushy mustache, flannel shirt instead of an Oxford, wool cap and jeans, always jeans, and asked who was sitting on the front lawn.

This possibility had not occurred to me. I had somehow believed that if I could just make it home I would be fine, that there was some sort of magic there, not to mention a semblance of safety. Yet this was clearly not the case. She was on the front lawn and I was now trapped in my own house. In a few short seconds I had traversed the thin line between freedom and house arrest.

What was I supposed to do? What if she didn't leave? Was it possible she would just take up camp there? And if so, what then? Might the neighbors start bringing her food and clothes? What if the newspapers picked up the story? Could this become a whole national movement? Of course it could and I could picture it all. Soon she would have pen pals and dignitaries coming by. Then celebrities would take up her cause and the Bob Dylan-types would write songs about her and perform them at folk festivals and benefits. It would be chaos and I would never be free again. These things happen of course, and when the momentum gets going what else can one do, but get caught up in the fervor and ultimately find oneself so overwhelmed by a force so much greater than yourself that you just give into to the inevitability all know is coming? I worried about all of this. And my stickball game of course.

It was all looking very bleak when I made a decision to do something that just a few years hence would not and could not be considered an acceptable option, I asked my dad for his advice. It was hard to discern whether or not he truly appreciated, or at least comprehended, the panic I was in, but he listened to me spell out the situation as I understood it. Then looking at me with the wisest face he could muster, and drawing on thousands of years of collective Jewish wisdom and erudition, he said with all sincerity, "Why don't you put on your Lone Ranger mask and walk right out the front door. If you're wearing a mask she won't even recognize you, right?"

It was brilliant, the perfect plan, and with that I put on my mask, walked out the front door, and without even pausing or looking in her direction, headed out into the night, not to think twice about her again that day or much after that at all.

She never followed me home again after that, and frankly, I don't know that I would ever have thought about her again, except for the fact that over the years my dad would mention from time to time how he had just run into her at the AM/PM Mini-Mart and that a casual sort of friendship between them had emerged following my early efforts to escape her.

26.

Full of turkey and nostalgia, I walk into Thirsty's and hunker down at the bar. I drink one Yuengling after another. I trace my finger along the empty bottles and watch the sweat collect on my finger before dripping onto the bar. I am able to not think about death and I am able now to do this for long stretches of the day. It doesn't feel right, but I can do it when properly distracted, which I am here, and now, as I focus on the bottle in front of me, and the label slowly sliding off and crumbling between my fingers.

This is doable, for hours even, and so it goes, order, drink, rinse, repeat. At some point I stop, because at some point I start to see double, and the people around me, start getting increasingly more blurry, merging into the furniture and into one another. I am in a fog, an alcohol induced fog, and the only thing that is clear to me right now is that I've never understood what it means to be in a metaphorical fog as well as I do at this time and at this moment.

I challenge myself to try and actually make out some of the faces drifting by me, ghostlike and amorphous. Can I distinguish the shape of someone's nose or identify the color of their eyes, or is everything now just a diffuse, shade of grey? I keep looking at everyone that walks by, I am staring, but I don't know anyone and I don't care. The question is whether I am still capable of thought and I think I am. Now, am I also capable of making decisions? That is less clear. Maybe I can test that as well?

I try to flag down the bartender, but I'm not sure whether I have raised my arm much less called out and tried to get his attention. I try again. Nothing. Not that I am convinced that I've done anything. I'm no longer sure what's action and what's merely thought. I'm just drifting now and it feels like it just might be time to put my head down and rest until I am ready to try again.

Moments, or is it hours, before I do though, she is by my side. I think it's her anyway. It's been a long time and I'm not all there.

"Is that you?" I ask her.

"It is," she says.

"Hey, Jessie, wow," I say feeling re-energized and re-focused, "you used to follow me home."

"Yes," she says.

She is like an apparition, luminescent and glowing as she hovers over me.

"Where did come from?" I ask. "Do you live here?"

"This is home," she says, "there were other places, but they didn't take. I'm sorry about your father by the way, we became friendly for awhile."

"I never understood that friendship," I say, "but I never understood him either, not really."

"Nothing's easy," she says.

"Maybe not," I say, "so, hey, can I take a turn following you home, or take you home, or something?"

"Why?" she says.

"Because I've been seeing ghosts all night," I say, "and I need to be with someone real."

"Fine," she says, "you can come home with me, but that doesn't mean you're not going home with a ghost."

"That's cool," I respond.

When I wake-up later that morning though, I trace my finger along the remaining streak of sweat on her bare shoulder to confirm she's real. After that I quickly get dressed, and then I walk out just like I did so many years before.

27.

I am on a plane and flying back to Chicago after visiting my dad. I am staring out the window. I can't quite think straight and I am talking to myself, or more accurately I am talking to my reflection which is hovering there in front of me, warped and undulating

"Here it is December all of a sudden," I say to myself, "and I'm thinking how great it would be to take some time off from this constant travel to the east coast to be with my dad. I'm also thinking that this may be okay because of the no doubt misguided, but nice if true, possibility that he somehow has more time left than projected. The thing is, he is somehow going strong and who knows, he may continue to do so because even while he failed to achieve a remission while at Johns Hopkins, he may very well have had some sort of mini-remission. He looks pretty good. His hair is coming back and it's even kind of coifed really. He's skinny and all, but he's got energy."

"Of course," I respond to myself, "if you were being honest with yourself, you would say that you doubt that he will continue to do well for all that long. That it is more accurate to acknowledge that you are just trying to convince myself that taking a month off from traveling home to visit your parents is okay, because frankly your dad's health may change at any time, and you know this. So, what you should really say is that you just want to take a break."

"Okay, fine," I say, "all this visiting is hard and I just wish I could slow down long enough to catch my breath. It's funny because I want to believe it is not hard and that I'm not tired or scared or sad or find visiting with him so draining at times because the discussion of no topic is complete until it has been fully exhausted from every possible angle."

"I get that," I reply, "but since you cannot change these things, what I will suggest is that since he is somehow still going, weaker, and somewhat more befuddled, but still going none-the-less, if you want to pretend just for now that he is healthy enough for you to take a break, I am going to give you that. I don't think it's true, and I know you know this, but you go with it, for now, okay?"

"Okay, thanks."

28.

My plane has landed. I have gathered my bags. I have walked down the long tunnel in O'Hare where the lights and sounds dance around my head with its beeps and swirls and the endless admonitions to mind the moving sidewalk. I have gotten on to the train and I have traveled back into the city. The city is dark and cold, with snow dancing around at my feet as I exit at Division and look for a cab that can take me the rest of the way home.

Kerri is waiting for me in bed, wanting to hear about every step I took and every conversation I had. I am in the bathroom though, beer in hand. I am leaning over the sink. I am staring into the mirror. The fluorescent light is terribly harsh and I can see every pore on my tired face, every scar, crevice and undulation. I have the beginnings of a double-chin and the first flecks of grey in my sideburns. I don't look as bad as I might though, worn down maybe, but not falling apart either, not by a long shot. I can live with this face.

I am not here to admire myself though. I am on a mission. I am studying my reflection, compulsively searching for ingrown hairs and exploring the day-old unshaven whiskers that populate my neck and face. I'm not sure when this started, but I know the drill, and I know I've grown more desperate about it since my father got sick.

I always begin my search just below my eyes, along my cheekbones, fanning out along my face towards my ears and then down towards my jaw line. At my jaw I tilt my face left and then right, tracing my jaw line from ear to chin before tilting my head back and looking across the taut expanse of my neck, from chin to collar bone.

The whiskers are different lengths here, twisted and ornery, some incredibly wispy, somehow having repeatedly escaped my razor's efforts to take them out. I don't know what causes ingrown hairs nor am I sure how to prevent them, what combination of shaving cream, balm, razor, hot water and technique will leave my skin blemish free. I do know that they have gotten worse with time. That age plays games with all body parts and bodily functions, with sudden allergies to milk, and increases in dandruff and nose hair. Worse though, or maybe, best for me are the whiskers. Where once the occasional ingrown hair would randomly appear, it's now a near daily problem, little bumps and irritations, the skin grown over a misshapen or misdirected hair, ugly markings dotting my neck and jowls. When I find a hair I see whether a quick pluck with the tweezers will break the skin and free it. Of course even if freed not all hair can be plucked. Hairs break. Blood is spilled. And sometimes I dig and dig, with nothing to show for my work, but a temporarily disfigured face and untrammeled anxiety now peaking with little hope of resolution in sight.

I usually lose myself in this right after work, and after these flights. It is a ritual now, and when successful, and a whisker actually comes free, the effect is incredibly calming, the day's stressors melting away. The hope is that doing this will soothe whatever errant thoughts are coursing through my head and stave off the inevitable anxieties at bedtime, especially when running, sex or massive amounts of alcohol are not readily available.

And so this is where I am now, in front of the mirror, standing in my boxers, doing a final scan and trying to mellow.

29.

My compulsions having been sated, Kerri and I are lying in bed. I am on my back and staring at the ceiling and she is curled up next to me as she studies my left arm. She begins tracing the scars that run along my forearm with her finger. They are now faded, but just barely.

"Tell me about your scars," Kerri says.

"Why," I reply, "you know the story."

"I want to take your mind off of your trip back home," she says, "and I want to take my mind off of worrying about you, so c'mon, tell me the story again."

And so I tell her the story.

How when I was eighteen years old I spent my summer doing odd jobs around town and that one afternoon I was scraping paint off of a neighbor's window when I fell off of the ladder I was on and dropped to the ground two floors below.

For a moment as I fell and stared into the sun above me, I wondered if this is what it felt like to die. First, a sense of weightlessness and then a lack of control, the feeling that I just might never stop falling, though even if I did I might still feel like I could never quite regain my balance. In the next moment, I wondered if I had already died, and if in fact I were in limbo, or getting ready to pass through the world as a ghost. If it was the latter, I wondered what that would be like. Could ghosts pass through walls? Or fly? Would I be able to enter any room unannounced, eavesdropping on conversations and at times looking at unsuspecting girls in their underwear? This could be fun, but what if I couldn't communicate with anyone? What if I had no relationships of any kind, and just endlessly drifted around? What then? What kind of existence was that?

Thud.

I am on the ground. I am not dead from what I can tell. However my left arm is simultaneously twisted in a number of directions. It is nauseating. The pain is sharp and endless, a thousand little knives driving themselves into my wrist, forearm and biceps, second after second after second. There is also a slow, trickle of blood coming from my nose, and dripping onto my sleeve. I want to stand-up, but I can't imagine placing my hand on the ground below me, much less moving my legs which seem to work, though I have no real desire to test this out.

"Aaaaaaaaaaaaaaaaaaaaaaaaaaah!"

There is a piercing scream coming from the porch. It is the daughter of the owner of the house and she is maybe sixteen, short brown hair and nice calves from what I can see. I try and a get a better angle on her breasts, but then she screams again and I remember what's going on. I have fallen from a ladder, my arm is broken and I may just have a concussion. Still, does that mean I am not supposed to be thinking about someone's breasts?

"Oh fuck. Oh fuck, oh fuck, oh fuck," she says coming down the stairs. "Should I call an ambulance? Or take you to the hospital? Can you stand? What happened?"

She leans over me and brushes the hair out of my face. I look down her tank-top.

"I think I can stand," I say. "Can you take me to the hospital?"

She can and she does. When I get to the hospital they ask me to sit down and tell me they will be with me shortly. I believe them, but they aren't telling the truth, they do not come back, not immediately, not at all. They are understaffed, and I have to sit there and rest my arm in my lap. Slowly, my arm starts to stiffen, and I want to move it, but then I picture the bones grinding together and so I don't move, not at all, I barely even breath, I just sit there, still, and not wanting to inflict any further damage.

At first, I'm cool, or tell myself I am anyway, no fear, no nothing. But somewhere along the way, as I sit there, alone, and untended to I start getting really freaked out and I start feeling really sorry for myself and I'm not sure how to get un-freaked out. And then the curtains part and there is my dad. He looks at me, and when he does, the sadness and shock quickly permeate the room. I look back at him, but neither of us say anything because what do you say at a time like this? Nothing, and so instead I just start to bawl. I haven't cried for at least ten years at this point, and I am ready to let it all out, all the tears I have skipped, and all the emotions I have suppressed.

"And why didn't you ever cry," Kerri says, "I can never remember that part."

"I don't know, I didn't, I thought not crying was cool, and I wanted nothing to do with it."

"You thought it was cool," she says. "Sometimes you're such a fucking guy."

"You think? Anyway, these are big tears, and I am nearly dry-heaving I'm crying so hard, and my dad, who never cried, just kind of stands there for a minute, unmoving and unsure of what to do or say."

"And?" Kerri says.

"And what, he finally says, you don't need to cry, and I say, I really do, and with that he walks over, grasps my good hand and lets me cry, neither of us saying another word until my mom arrives."

"That's like right out of a movie," Kerri says sitting-up, "and in that movie I picture you being played by River Phoenix and your dad being played by Judd Hirsch."

"Of course you do," I say, "meanwhile, what happened to the idea that you were going take my mind off of home?"

30.

The therapist is looking at me with that curly hair. And those hands, those tiny little hands that I want to suck on. She's not talking, so I am not talking. I will speak before her though and she knows this. Not that it's a game to her. This is about giving me space and allowing me to get in touch with myself, right?

"I am consistently struck by the fact that I can consistently go to work and be productive and basically go through the day like nothing major is going on in my life," I start to say to her. "I have this ability to compartmentalize my world and say to myself that being at work is about being at work and this crazy shit with my dad is not going to interfere with my day. Everyone at the office knows what's going on and they are all very supportive and they ask questions, but they do not press or pry all that much and so there it is, I'm busy, but supported, distracted by my dad, but equally distracted by work, and I just keep kind of plugging along. The thing is where do I get off being so composed or focused or reserved or whatever during the day? Is this not a major tragedy that deserves tears or the inability to concentrate or something?"

"What do you think?" she asks.

"I don't know, I don't think it helps that there are those in my life who find this ability to compartmentalize admirable or impressive. Such admiration only reinforces the idea that this is good or righteous behavior though. Of course even as I recognize this, even as I'm saying it to you, do I do anything about it? No, and why is this, because while being tough is very important to me, being perceived as tough is probably just as important."

"So?" the therapist says, her big eyes, round and welcoming, her hands scribbling notes, her hands, that I wish were rubbing my neck, my shoulders, my temples, everything.

"So, I want to feel bad about all this. Well I think I do. Well, I definitely want people to think I feel bad. Of course do I do anything that will let them know this? No, what would I do? I don't know how to answer that, then again maybe that is the real problem any way. I am not embarrassed that I can compartmentalize, I'm just embarrassed that people recognize I can and this somehow doesn't seem right to me."

"Good," the therapist says, "that's a good insight, we can build on that."

"I guess, you know, the irony of course, is that there are those moments, especially when I slow down during the day, or some Springsteen song comes on the radio, or who knows what will happen, maybe nothing at all, when I just get so sad while sitting at my desk, I cannot move, or work, or do anything, I'm paralyzed. No one ever sees me like that though, and I don't plan to let them do so."

"Never?" she says.

"No, never."

And with that, her hands float away and I try to follow them.

31.

My father never seemed to sleep. He would say that sleep was the enemy. That there was never enough time to get everything done even if it seemed he always had all the time in the world to get these things done when compared to the dads who were going to work in an office somewhere all day, lost to some cubicle or office park, wearing ill-fitting suits, dealing with office politics, idiot bosses and long commutes to and from work.

My father had a studio where he wrote and painted and shared with tattoo artists. He wore jeans everyday of his adult life. He rode an Italian racing bike around town when he wasn't walking and during that magical time of the day when my mother was at work and my brother and I were at school he was free to follow his muses wherever they took him.

But it was never enough time, which meant he was inevitably awake and prowling around the house well into the night, some times working, drawing or writing, but more likely thinking about this lack of time as he sat cross-legged on the couch with Nebraska, the White Album or Desire quietly playing in the background. He was also likely smoking a pipe with a cup of coffee looming off on the table. He was probably reading a copy of *The Nation*, *Tikkun*, *Cineaste* or *Art Forum*. And he was definitely lost in thought, and lost in the endless possibilities of work still to be done and undone.

As I lie here in my old room, visiting home again, and unable to sleep, I realize I've become my father. And as I walk downstairs to get a drink of water I see him sitting on the couch reading, which is how I would find him whatever time it was I got home as a kid, home from late night runs, dates or parties, sitting there on the couch, no more than one or two lights on across the first floor of the house.

He wasn't always easy to talk to then. Well, ever. That's not accurate. It's easier now, but back then he wasn't always easy to connect with. He could always talk, but sharing in pain and fears, even joy, those feelings weren't always accessible.

Still, during those late nights, stripped-down, removed from family, work and whatever struggles that accompanying those things, it was different, if only briefly. It was a safe place, a demarcated zone where any conversation was possible, though they might only last a few minutes, because I was still an adolescent and with that role comes the necessary deniable plausibility. Even if I had the opportunity to talk to a parent, and even if I wanted to, it doesn't mean I allowed myself to do so. It's just not done.

And I know I could go talk to him now, but I pause, he seems peaceful and I wonder if talking to him might not initiate some random agitation he's trying to get away from. I realize though, that this just might be my own projection, that while I might not be able to sleep, that doesn't mean that I want to get agitated either.

I decide not to get that drink of water, or even talk to my dad. I just go back upstairs and climb into bed. Not that I sleep. I just get nostalgic and sad.

Years ago, Kerri and I went to go see the movie *Running on Empty* with River Phoenix. In it he played the older son in a family that has been on the run from the law ever since setting a napalm lab on fire during the Vietnam War, moving from home to home, and town to town, changing identities and moving always moving. At the time the movie takes place, the River Phoenix character is thinking about whether it is time to carve out his own life, though this comes at the risk of maybe never seeing his family again. The father is played by Judd Hirsch and there is this scene where River Phoenix comes home late one night from a date and his father is sitting on the couch and they sort of have this moment, no tension, no bullshit, just a moment, a moment that seemed to capture my childhood better than anything I had ever seen on film.

When River Phoenix died on the sidewalk outside of The Viper Room following an overdose, something died in me as well. River Phoenix had always represented to me the need to separate from your family if you ever hoped to grow and be something unique and independent, but then to die like that, on the street, and so far from home, it seemed hard to believe that separating had ever seemed so important to me, or at least that anyone is truly rewarded with the kind of benefits I hoped separating would impart. Of course, River Phoenix was playing a character, but that hadn't mattered to me then, and it didn't matter to me when he died, because when he died I had to question everything, and who wants to do that?

32.

It's the end of the day and I'm on the train platform, a Venti, Starbucks skinny double-shot on ice in one hand, the sports page in the other, my Walkman firmly in place and Bruce Springsteen accompanying me on the ride home.

"Last night I dreamed that I was a child out where the pines grow wild and tall—I was trying to make it home through the forest before the darkness falls—I heard the wind rustling through the trees and ghostly voices rose from the fields—I ran with my heart pounding down that broken path—With the devil snappin' at my heels—I broke through the trees, and there in the night— My father's house stood shining hard and bright the branches and brambles tore my clothes and scratched my arms—But I ran till I fell, shaking in his arms."

Kerri has told me that I shouldn't tune out like this, that I don't pay enough attention to my surroundings when I do, and that things can happen. I usually ignore her as I am doing today, and so I don't see Jessie and Rhoda come up the stairway to the platform, nor do I see him leave her side and walk down to the far end of the platform where I am waiting for the train, much less notice him trying to talk to me.

"Hey, hey man, what the fuck?"

Jessie is standing right in front of me. I haven't seen him and Rhoda for weeks. They haven't been coming by the office and no one has run into them on the street or in the park.

"I'm trying to talk to you?"

My chest tightens and a sense of panic spreads everywhere starting with my groin and crashing into the back of my head. I try to be cool.

"What up," I say to him, "how about we talk tomorrow in the office?"

"I don't think so."

I step back. He leans in.

"You were hitting on Rhoda the last time we were in the office," he says, "and that's why we haven't been back. I want that shit to stop."

I back up again. I need some distance between the two of us.

"Maybe you misunderstood something," I say, "I was just doing my job and Rhoda was hanging out, and it was nothing, really."

"The fuck it was," he says, "I saw the way you were looking at her, and the way she was looking at you. Don't lie to me."

He leans in even further. There isn't much platform behind me and what's left is getting narrower. I wonder if I'm going to have to fight Jessie, something that fills me with dread and anticipation all at once. Jessie leans forward again and I picture punching him as hard as I can. I feel a surge of adrenalin, even as I feel shaken by the very thought of it. Someone is going to have to make some kind of move though and they are going to have to do so soon.

The train suddenly appears, as suddenly as Jessie did moments before. I jump on as the doors open and as the doors close I see Jessie staring at me through the windowpanes. The train starts to pull away and I'm gone, into the darkness and breathing hard until I get home.

33.

The world just keeps moving, ever faster, and ever more complex despite, or maybe it is in spite, of my father's illness doing everything it can to take center stage in my most unstable of universes. It is hard enough trying to get a handle on what I think I know and then boom, right in the middle of all this comes *Magnolia*, like a thunderbolt, or maybe more appropriately, like a deluge a frogs from the sky above.

Kerri has been out drinking with her friends and I have been at the movies with Marcus and Bryan this other guy from the office. We are in bed, Kerri is curled-up on my chest and I can smell a mixture of spearmint toothpaste and Vodka emanating from her mouth with each light breath.

"So what was it about?" Kerri asks half-awake.

"Everything," I say, "It's this Altmanesque riff on not just all the ways we can be horrible to each other, and all the ways the world can let us down, but all the ways we try to seek closure, pleasure and reconciliation."

"Can you be more specific? Does anything actually happen?"

"Yes, of course, there's this cop who can't find love and falls for this fucked-up woman who was raped by her father as a kid."

"You're so not selling it."

"Wait, and there is her father, Jimmy Gator, this famous television personality who is dying and just wishes he could make good with her. You have the Anthony Robbins-like sex guru played by Tom Cruise, whose father Big Earl left him as a boy. The sex guru would just as soon have nothing to do with him, but Big Earl is dying as well and his nurse reaches out to the son hoping he will come pay one last visit so Big Earl can make amends before his death."

"Sounds like fun."

"Right, it was really fucking painful to watch," I say, "but what's really throwing me is that Marcus and Bryan found it hopeful. They focused on its message about the power of forgiveness and I can't argue with them because hope does lurk on the periphery of the movie. But it is definitely the periphery, fighting for attention along with the messages about damaged families, anger, poor behavior, death and regret, which resonated loudest for me because I couldn't help but think about my grandmother and now father, their battles with regret as their lives deserted them, and the idea that like the characters of Jimmy Gator or Big Earl Partridge there is no peace for the dying."

"Why should your dad be at peace given his age and the randomness of it all?" Kerri asks. "This sucks for him, for you and your mom, all of you."

"I know," I say, "but why does he have to carry so much regret at the end, or at least why has he had to get this far still carrying so much? I know regret and anger if invited are only too happy to follow you on your life's journey, and stand to only be exacerbated at the end of that journey if not discarded or reconciled along the way. And I know we all make choices on this journey, and the bad ones, and the ones we know to be wrong, will haunt us, if not immediately, then when we look back and no longer have any control over them, but there has to be some relief at some point doesn't there?"

"Dude, you're getting really worked-up, and I'm sorry, and I love you, but it's late…"

"One more thing," I say ignoring her pleas. "There is another truth here as well. Big Earl was given just enough time to find peace, and my dad has time as well. He is still going strong, despite what they tell him he should be feeling and where he should be. And so given that, maybe there is still some hope yet."

"Of course there is, and now I'm going to sleep," she says kissing me on the cheek.

I watch her drift off and think about how's she mostly right, isn't she? Hope does loom large. I couldn't make it though the day, or at least feel like I was remotely in control of my day without it. And sure, to some extent pretending is what makes hope possible for me, but maybe that's why I struggled so much to find anything positive in *Magnolia*.

I'm always looking to be hopeful, and even try to convince myself I am hopeful, but when it comes down to it I'm just not quite sure I really believe it.

Marcus and Bryan though are believers. They believe there are greater forces at play, but I don't, I only see darkness and destruction.

I get out of bed and lace up my running shoes.

34.

We all sit back, my mom, dad, Kerri and myself, kicking it at my parent's house, visions of Denzel Washington dancing in our heads while we listen to the story of Hurricane Carter on a scratchy old vinyl version of *Desire*, reminiscing and talking music, movies and mortality.

"Do you remember when we bought this album?" my mom says.

"In New York City on that trip, right," my dad responds, "we bought it on the street, brand new, right?"

"Yes," my mom says, "it cost $1.50 and you wondered if it was worth paying that much for it."

"Do you ever wonder how those street vendors manage to get all that brand new stuff?" Kerri says.

"Better not to question it," I reply, "just think of it as a public service."

Everyone laughs and for a moment we all relax and listen to Dylan. And then we get quiet. For even with the afterglow of hope still kind of washing over us, reality has settled back in. There are rising blast counts in my father's peripheral blood and low platelet and red blood counts as well. There is fatigue. And there will be no waiting until spring to visit Johns Hopkins. He will go soon, he will stay and we will hope for the best.

It's funny, because just as I start to let myself forget, it's back, the truth and the reality. Like a blow from Hurricane Carter, it is in our faces again and again, unrelenting, no time to duck, no time to move. And there may be a lesson here. We cannot forget what we are dealing with, we should not give up hope, not ever, but we cannot forget, not for one day, not for one moment that this disease is fatal if not treated.

My father may yet be saved, the bone marrow donor drives being held on his behalf may unearth a still to be discovered donor, and modern science may still open some door, but there are no miracles here, it just doesn't work like that.

And while I know this, I think about the Hurricane and I have to ask, is this justice? I think not. Of course does justice even have anything to do with this? Is disease just, a form of retribution for past wrongs and misdeeds? I don't believe so, or at least I don't want to believe so, because if I did I might have to question my father's decisions and actions along the way which is something I'm not ready to do.

35.

Kerri has gone to sleep as have my parents. I think about strapping on my running shoes, heading out into the late night, maybe going down to the track and running lap after lap, alone and focused on one step, then the next and then the one after that, losing myself in the darkness and quiet, far from sickness and death and fear and sadness as I become one with the universe.

Well, this is what I might have done. Instead, I get into the car and start driving around. I cruise the mostly quiet streets, passing one house after another, the lights off except for the occasionally flickering television tuned into whatever it is people watch at this time at night, most likely old episodes of Seinfeld and QVC.

I know there are maybe a million things to think about and reflect on, but I decide a drink is the best way to go, and maybe not just one drink either. I drift down to Thirsty's and wonder if I was planning on coming here all along.

It's late and Thirty's is mostly empty, except for the usual handful of hardcore, late night drunks hunkered down around the bar, looking to forget as much as possible before stumbling home and preparing to come back the next day.

I also wonder if I will see Jessie the lawn girl, but I go to the far end of the bar and I am ready to hunker down myself when I spot someone I once new in high school sitting alone at a corner booth and methodically working his way through a pitcher of beer. I haven't seen him since graduation, but I have heard that he has been wildly successful, moving from

Georgetown undergrad to law school at Penn, a big job in New York City and now back at home and working for his father's firm as he raises his family in the calming environs of upstate New York.

I assume he will want to talk and laugh about high school, talk about the girls we wished we had fucked and riff on the relative merits of the John Hughes oeuvre.

I walk over.

"Hey man," I say, "what up, it's been a long time."

"Yeah it has been a long time," he says, barely looking-up.

"How have you been," I ask, "is everything all right?"

"Like you give a fuck," he says.

Then he looks at me, and he is angry, angry at me, at something I did, or didn't do, something I represent, or don't. I don't know and I don't know him, probably never did.

"Where's the love," I say forcing a smile, "how about I get some more beer, and we can talk. What do you think?"

He pauses, grimaces, and tries to concentrate. The alcohol is wreaking havoc with his ability to focus on much besides the hatred that is oozing out of his pores like the beer he's drinking will do when he wakes up wherever it is he collapses on nights like this.

"You and your fucking friends," he says his voice rising, "your goddamn high school clique, too good to talk to anyone, just drinking and fucking and running around like you owned the place. And now you want to talk to me? Well fuck you. I've spent ten years forgetting about people like you, and now you're in my bar walking around like you own this place. Like you belong here, fuck you, you don't."

No one has ever spoken to me like this. No one has ever felt this much hatred towards me. Have they? Meanwhile, is he right about me and who I was? That wasn't me back then, was it? No, it couldn't be, I got along with everyone. Didn't I?

"Hey, look," I say wondering if we might come to blows, "high school was a long time ago, and if I was a dick, I apologize, but do you want to drink or not, because I'm here to drink."

He looks at me again, and starts to relax.

"So what do you do?" he says.

"I work with the homeless," I say.

"Really?'

"Yeah, really."

"That's cool," he says smiling, and whatever was going on between us is done, not that I'm sure why, maybe it's because he thinks I'm doing good now and I can absolved of my behavior as a teenager, or maybe he thinks he's doing better than me. Then again, maybe it doesn't matter, because why should this make any more sense than anything else?

"So, are you going to get us another pitcher or what?" he says.

"Sure, yes, for sure."

And then we drink.

36.

I wake-up hung-over and skuzzy. I pry my head off of the pillow. I wander downstairs and as I cross through the dining room I see my mom in the kitchen, her back to me, drinking coffee and reading the paper. As I look at her in the kitchen, the new kitchen, the one with the nice stone-tiled floors and new cabinets, I flash back to the old kitchen, the kitchen we had when I was a kid, and as I think about it, I also flash back to a scene from that time, something I haven't thought about in years.

I was seven years old and I was playing hockey with my neighbor in his garage. We were totally into it, getting loud and knocking things over, when his dad suddenly appeared out of nowhere and yelled at us for making too much noise. Shortly after that I learned that my neighbor's dad was leaving his mom and I asked my mother if it was because we had been too noisy. She told me that people didn't leave each other for reasons like that. She didn't tell me, however, why people did.

Who knows now what I was thinking exactly when I asked her this, but I know I must have been on to something, because it wasn't long after that that my father left home for the first time. I remember that he and my mom asked me to sit down in the kitchen so I could talk. The kitchen had red flowered wallpaper then and yellow benches built into the wall around the table. The benches were especially cool because they doubled as storage containers and were great for hiding things.

Anyway, they sat me down and told me how my father was moving out for a little while, but that things would be the same, and that I'd still see him as much as I ever did. I remember sitting there trying to look real nonchalant and unbothered by the news, staring straight ahead the whole time, no emotions, no nothing. They asked if I if I had any questions, but I didn't say a word, choosing instead to casually shake my head no, focused on getting out and moving on before the tears came.

Now why it all went down this way is hard to say, because I certainly could have asked my dad why he was leaving, or how we had all gotten to this point. But I didn't. And someone maybe could have asked me how I felt about all that was happening. And maybe they did. But I don't remember it like that.

No, what I remember, is that when he moved back home, and left again, or when he came by the house long enough to make dinner, I never did ask him why he or anyone else chose to leave. I wondered, but I also wondered why people stayed together when it seemed to cause them so much pain.

Maybe it was easier not to know. Or maybe it was just easier to convince myself that none of it had any affect on me because I always believed that was the case and no one ever told me different.

37.

It's late, which is nice, dark, which is really nice, and I am back in Chicago and running along the lakefront, the water still, the wind mild, the possibilities endless. The idea is to not think, to get a break from that, but it's not going to happen, not tonight, tonight I have too much on my mind not to think, and with every step I take, and with every effort to think of other things, how my legs feel, how Kevin Spacey's performance in *American Beauty* compares to Denzel Washington's in *The Hurricane*, and on and on, I keep coming back to my head and the clutter and soon enough I'm talking to myself.

"False starts and false hopes, it's all we have, right?" I say to myself. "Sure I have work and that isn't so bad. It has been an amazingly mild winter so far, and so that isn't so bad either. And so, I guess I'm doing alright as far as those kinds of things go. On the other hand, the Dow is down, so very down, a correction or something and Northern Ireland is in the same place as Syria and Israel. Bill Bradley's campaign is not in great shape and I'm not sure how I feel about that. Hillary is not doing so well right now either, and since Guliani is to blame, I'm quite sure how I feel about that."

"If you don't mind me asking," I ask myself, "why are you always riffing on popular, political and world happenings, and why are you so flippant about it?"

"That's a good question," I respond, "I guess it all has something to do with time in general, and lost time in particular. How I have entered the world of the diseased and in this world time ceases to exist in so many ways. Days are lost in the hospital; the weeks begin to merge together, a series of intertwined phone calls, transfusions, and flights; and entire months disappear as potential treatments are sought and lost. Without these sorts of updates and news flashes it would be so easy to believe that the world itself has stopped moving, and that my dad's illness is all that is going on anywhere."

"But of course it is not," I say, "the world does not stop for any man, not even your dad."

"Exactly, so on another note, how can it be that he can be dying and the world is not taking notice on any level in any way? It is so very big to me, and so all consuming, how can't everyone feel that way? And more importantly, how can a Senate race seem remotely important in comparison?"

"Yeah, I don't know what to say to that," I say to myself, "it must be very hard to make sense of these things."

"It is, but then, there are so many things I cannot make sense of. There was this possibility that the University of South Carolina was going to come to my dad's rescue just like the Thalidomide people in Chicago had promised to do before them. Oh yes, you must come down to Columbia, they said. We're ready to do a mismatched, less then perfect donor kind of thing. We will even use bone marrow from one of your brothers, or maybe one of your kids if possible. And you want to believe them, because it's all so seductive. Here I've been wondering what if anything is possible and there they are telling us that anything is possible. Sure the fatality rate is like 80%, but if he makes it through that first year, who knows. And who knew, but it was something else to believe in."

"And," I say.

"And what," I respond, "you know what I am going to say next, the doctors in South Carolina won't treat him, too dangerous, too futile. Never mind that over the phone they insisted he come on down, or that he feels pretty good, because those counts keep moving along. So, it's back to Hopkins, though they don't offer hope, just time. Time for me to spend with my father whether he wants more time or not and time to keep deluding myself, though there will never be enough time for that."

And then I stop talking to myself, I have talked it out, and whether or not I feel any better is beside the point, there is nothing left to say right now. I can run though, into the night, into the dark, swallowed-up by the big sky above me and the vast lake beside me, a lone figure, slowly disappearing into my head and then into the universe around me.

38.

I am at Moody's Pub with Marcus and Bryan. Bryan and I are consuming one bottle of Leinenkugel Red after another. Marcus is drinking club soda. They have taken me out because they know about my dad and want to check-in with me. They also want to be sure I am taking care of myself.

"I really appreciate the concern," I say polishing off another bottle of Leinie and beckoning for the waitress, "but I'm cool. My dad is going back to Hopkins and we will see what happens."

"Look man, we don't want to pry," Marcus says, "you just seem a little too cool, you know?"

"Which is fine, we guess," Bryan adds, "but it's also a little unnerving, you don't seem to be, I don't know, all that emotional."

I could tell them I don't try to do emotional, especially at work, but that would be rude, they really seem to care.

I decide to tell them a story instead.

"Okay," I say, "so I was like ten years old when I went to see *The Champ* with my friend Joey Wallace. You know that movie, right?"

Bryan is way too young to know anything about *The Champ*, but Marcus will know.

"I got nothing," Bryan says.

"Is that the boxing movie?" Marcus asks.

"Right," I say, "Jon Voight is an ex-boxer and kind of a loser and his ex-wife is this rich chick played by Faye

Dunaway. His young son is played by Ricky Schroeder and Ricky wants him to start boxing again."

"I remember that," Marcus says. "So he decides to fight again, but when it comes time to actually fight someone he gets really fucked-up, right?"

"Yes," I respond, "and after the fight they lay him on a table in the dressing room and he's dying and Ricky starts hitting Jon Voight's chest with his little fists, crying and screaming 'Champ' over and over again. But it doesn't help, because the motherfucker dies, just like that, even as Ricky tries to will him back to life."

"I bawled during that scene," Marcus says, "my brother made fun of me for weeks after that."

"Exactly, of course you bawled, that scene is killer, and when I saw it I really thought that I was going to cry as well. I wanted to cry, but I didn't, I just wouldn't let myself do so. And while I probably never would have cried in front of Joey anyway, the real problem wasn't that I was there with him, but the fact that back then I would have never let myself cry at all regardless of the circumstances."

"I don't get it," Bryan says, "you didn't cry as a kid?"

"No, I wanted to be tough."

"And that's it?" Marcus asks.

"No," I respond, "not at all, that's the thing, my dad never fucking cried at all. I can only remember having seen him cry once and that was at his father's funeral. We were out at this ancient cemetery in Queens or Long Island and it was this blustery day, and my dad was standing next to his two younger brothers and they were reading some passage in Hebrew. When my dad's turn came his face contorted in a way I had never seen and then the tears came, grudgingly, and without ease, but they came, and it wasn't pretty. It was terrible and it was just that one time and I think I just decided that I would never be like that, not if I could help it anyway."

"What about now though?" Bryan asks.

"Yeah, you're not a little kid anymore," Marcus says.

"I don't know," I say, "now that my dad's sick, I realize that it wasn't just about being tough for him. I don't think he was comfortable being around tears at all, because tears are raw and painful and I'm not sure he could bear to be around that kind of pain. I don't think I'm ready to be around that kind of pain either. Not mine, not his, not anyone's."

"You might want to work on that," Marcus says.

"Indeed," I respond.

39.

There is a groan, and inhuman groan that I initially ignore as I am lost in my parent's medicine cabinet and childhood memories. I am staring at the endless array of medicine, bandages and random medical supplies that now dominate the medicine cabinet, shelves and every spare spot left over.

Growing-up, there were only two items in the medicine cabinet outside of my father's rusty razor, an ancient bottle of Bayer aspirin that kicked around for years, and some sort of body-cleansing colonic that I don't believe anyone actually used.

There is another groan and now I'm kind of scared, but I do not budge.

The fact is, my father was always resistant to medical care, something which is causing me a lot of cognitive dissonance now, because since my father was diagnosed with the myelodisplasia he has done everything possible to find a cure and find the right doctors, endlessly asking questions to anyone who will listen.

One time when I was kid, my parents took Jerry and I on a trip to see an old friend of theirs in some backwater upstate New York town. There was a lake there that we all went swimming in and my dad stepped on a rusty nail.

He insisted he was fine and that there was nothing to worry about. But he wasn't, and there was, and on the following Monday afternoon when my mom stopped by the house she found him huddled on the couch, wrapped in blankets and running an incredibly high temperature. When she insisted on taking him to the hospital he said he was fine and refused medical attention between shivers.

She took him to the hospital anyway, and when they got there they found out that his foot was infected and that he had risked amputation if he had waited much longer.

He ended up staying in the hospital for two weeks and initially I smile at the inanity of the memory, but then I hear another groan emanating from my parent's bedroom and I realize I need to act, not sure why I haven't already.

"What's going on," I ask my dad through the closed door.

"I'm having a problem with my hernia," he responds breathlessly and clearly in pain.

He first told me about the hernia problem several years ago and for awhile I pestered him about getting it repaired before I finally dropped it because he kept saying he planned to do so soon. Now I learn that he never did anything.

"Jesus, how can you bear to be in this kind of discomfort while you're receiving chemotherapy and everything else? Get it fucking fixed already?" I say less than nicely through the still closed door.

For a moment he doesn't say a word and I just shake my head.

"It's too late," he finally says. "The cancer is so far along they can no longer operate on it."

I want to be empathic, and in my head I am. Really I am. But I also realize that there are many things about him that I'm just not sure exactly how to feel about. Someone leaves home, but comes back, only to leave again, and it's confusing, but I don't know remember what I thought then about it or what I think even now. The hernia though is different, because in this case I know exactly how I feel, furious, totally fucking furious, no confusion, no second guessing and no back pedaling.

I am angry that he could have treated himself like this, but I am also angry that he could treat our family like this as well, because in this moment I realize that his decisions, and non-decisions, don't just affect him, they affect all of us, and they always did.

40.

How do you remember someone when they are gone, especially when you're not sure how well you know them? This question has been haunting me lately and so I have decided that I need to get my father on tape talking about his life.

I have my father sit in the old rocking chair by the fireplace and in front of the mantle, the mantle that no one ever bothered to fully attach, which means that to this day you lean on it at your own risk, because it will tip and photos will fall. This doesn't seem as important today as it once did, though it does somehow remind me that the world is fragile and that at times all it takes is a misplaced elbow for it to be moved off its axis and crumble around your feet.

I set-up the tripod, spreading the legs apart, trying to ensure they are of equal lengths, the correct height and balance. I fumble with the video camera, trying to fasten it to the top of the tripod, attempting to straighten it out and be sure it is the right height. I try to determine if I am too close and if the shot is focused. I walk myself through the instructions on how to record and look for the red light that means I am actually doing so.

I ask my father some basic questions about his childhood, his parents and siblings, the neighborhood and being Jewish in the New York City of the 1940's and 50's.

My dad is answering my questions, and while he is articulate, he is lacking energy, slumping more with each passing minute, his hands resting in his lap.

I wonder if we should take a break and give him a rest, but I selfishly worry that this may be it, he may have less energy when I return to this project and after that who knows whether he will be here at all. I then ask him about his favorite memory as a child.

"Going to the Metropolitan Museum of Art," he says. "It was magical. It was an escape from the claustrophobic confines of my home and neighborhood. After being there I knew what I was going to do with my life. It was set. I was going to be an artist of some kind and knowing this was liberating. It wasn't clear to me how I would pull it off, but that didn't matter, a switch had been flipped and I was on a path, a path that I never left regardless of what else I had to do and regardless of the distractions I encountered."

As he says this, the color returns to his cheeks, and he becomes animated, his shoulders squared, his hands gesticulating. He has been reborn and the afternoon suddenly melts away before us.

41.

After the video camera has been packed-up for the day and my parents have gone to sleep. And after I have run up and down the hills and then around the track until I feel almost normal, I drift into the bathroom for a quick survey of my face, shower and head out into the night.

Thirsty's is packed tonight with an endless array of faces I do not recognize. I hunker down at the bar with a pitcher of Yuengling and watch the masses ebb and flow, drinking, swaying, talking, laughing and always moving and morphing, like my reflection on the glass in front of me, warped like a carnival mirror and mocking me for being alone, confused and desperate.

The crowd shifts, a small group of women emerge from it and there she is, Jessie, the lawn girl, her curly hair swaying about and splayed across her shoulders. I watch her talk and smile and wonder if, when, she will look at me, and then when she does, what she will do, will she walk over and maybe mouth something to me, only to me, about meeting outside or later or who knows what.

For awhile she doesn't turn, but finally she looks to the bar and we make eye contact. She smiles and tips her drink my way, but that's it, no movement, no words, just a smile and on with her evening.

This is good though. I don't want to want her, or be with her, I should be done with this, even just the idea of it. How did I become this guy?

And then she is standing there.

"Hey," she says, "you don't come over and say hello?"

"You seemed to be having fun," I say, "plus I didn't really get the sense that you wanted me to."

"Look man," she says, "you walked out on me, again, last time we got together, which is fine, but if you want me, you need to come to me, if you don't, cool, there are no strings and no expectations here, but I won't do all of the work either."

There is no such thing as no strings and no expectations, sex doesn't work like that and I know this as surely as I know anything. But why not go for it one more time, and then I will be done with it, all of it.

Later as we lie there in her bed and as I fight every inclination I have to run, she faces me and strokes my cheek with her fingers. This is what expectations looks like, or at least how it starts.

42.

Back home. I have done my usual rituals. I have walked the tunnel in the airport. I have taken the train home. I have stood in the bathroom under the hot glare of the lights over the medicine cabinet and search my face for bumps and trapped hairs. I stop in the bedroom to see Kerri who is long asleep and looks so peaceful I choose not to wake her.

I have not gone running though, I am too tired and my running shoes though just across the room seem miles away and impossible to reach. Instead I am sitting on the couch in the dark, eyes half-open, sipping a beer and trying to relax.

Rinnnnnnnnng.

I snap to attention, fully awake, eyes now open, beer dripping into my lap.

Rinnnnnnnnng.

What the fuck is that?

Rinnnnnnnnng.

I start looking around.

Rinnnnnnnnng.

It's the phone. Of course, it's the phone, but who calls at this time of night?

"Hello."

"Hello?"

"Hey man, its Jerry, how did things go with dad this week?"

"Jerry, hey, sorry I was dozing off here. How did it go?"

I think about telling Jerry how earlier today I rode in the first train car on the way home from the airport and as

I did I watched a father hold his young boys up to the front window as we sped into the unknown. The kids looked like they felt safe and warm and completely thrilled. And the dad looked proud, and caring, and a little thrilled as well, as he watched the world through their eyes. After I smiled all I wanted to do was cry, wondering what the world looks like when you no longer have a dad that is part of it.

I don't tell Jerry this story though and I'm not sure if that's because I want to protect him or myself, I just know there is enough sadness and everything doesn't have to feel so sad all the time.

"It went fine," I say, "you know how it is."

And he does. And then we both get quiet.

"Hey, how about I call you back tomorrow," I say, "when I'm more awake?"

"Of course, get some sleep bro, tomorrow, no problem."

We hang-up and I drift off right there on the couch dreaming about dads and trains and memories that stay good until everything starts to go bad.

43.

At some point I pull myself off of the couch and head into our room. I try to be quiet, but Kerri wakes up the second I hit the bed, wanting to know everything, and so we end up curled into fetal position and staring at each other, practically touching noses.

"How did the taping go?" she asks.

"Decent, he was tired most of the time, but he had his moments."

"How tired, did you guys shoot pool?"

"One day, it wasn't good though. One game I actually ran the table. And that was after I had already beat him like five straight times. It was not fun. It was more like a slaughter. Like when Larry Holmes fought Tex Cobb. No like when Holmes fought Ali, Tex Cobb actually tried to hit him back."

"Huh?"

"It was horrible."

"I'm sorry."

"I know and I love you for that."

"Did you sleep with anyone while you were home?"

I pause, but just briefly.

"No," I reply, which is not true, but I wish it was.

"Good."

"I think so."

"I was joking."

"I knew that."

"So," she says.

"So?"

Why does that make me nervous?

"I saw this report on Today show," she says, "about how you can sometimes use the cord blood from a baby for bone marrow transplants and I was thinking that if we had a baby your dad could possibly benefit from that."

"Wow, that's a fucked-up way of trying to get me to have a baby with you," I say trying to be funny and not freaked-out by every single implication of what she's saying.

"I know that freaks you out, but we are going to have a baby at some point anyway, right?"

"Absolutely," I say as firmly as I can, because we are going to, I know this and even look forward to it, though maybe not at the moment, "but I don't know, what if he dies before the baby is born, or worse, what if it doesn't work, and I think the chances are really unlikely from what I've read, we then have to raise a baby even as he's dying. Are we ready for that?"

"I don't know," she says sadly, "I just want to save his life."

"I know you do, and so do I, but I don't think this is the way."

"Okay, I know that."

And maybe she does, but do I really know that, or am I just being a scared and selfish bastard that just signed his father's death sentence?

44.

Marcus and I are at Marie's Golden Cue up on Montrose after work. It's dim inside, which is fine, because we are here to shoot pool and that is it, shoot pool and think about nothing but that, no dad, no disease, no nothing, just pool.

Well, that and chicks, but that's it.

I have a five ball sitting on the bumper near a corner hole. It's not a gimme, but if I make it, the eight ball is waiting for me and its game over, do not pass go, do not collection two-hundred dollars. I line it up. It feels right. I shoot. I start moving towards the eight ball.

"Dude," Marcus says, "you missed."

Huh? I did miss. The five is sitting on the lip of the hole, and still quivering Caddyshack-style, but without the requisite explosions necessary to nudge it in. Where's Bill Murray when you need him? Marcus then proceeds to drop the nine, the eleven, the fifteen and then the eight. Game over.

"My dad and I call that the Tony moment," I tell Marcus as I begin to rack.

"The Tony moment, what the fuck are you talking about" Marcus responds as he goes to break.

"The Tony moment," I say "is the moment during a game of pool when you're playing someone of equal or greater skill, particularly greater skill, and after you have taken the lead, you miss the shot that would have clinched the game for you. Well, it feels like it would have clinched the game for you. But you've missed it, and having done so it opens a window of opportunity for your opponent that moments earlier seemed closed. What clinches its status as a Tony moment, is that your opponent, having been given this new lease on life, not only avoids making the kind of mistake you just have, but also sinks the shot or shots needed to win the game."

"And why is the Tony moment," Marcus says sinking the two and four before missing the six, "why not the Marcus moment?"

"We were talking about this dude Tony when we coined the phrase. He is the best player either of us has ever seen," I say as I sink the fourteen and then miss the ten.

"I'm as good as Tony," Marcus says missing the six again.

"No offense," I say, "but I knew Tony, and you're no Tony. The Tony's are able to seize any opportunity that presents itself. And, to seize it is not just them recognizing the fact that an opportunity suddenly exists, but it is also their possessing the ability to then concentrate on that opportunity so intently that they cannot or will not allow themselves to fail. You're good, but you're not that good. Guys like Tony don't just concentrate more intently then everyone else, they're playing a different game."

"Fuck," Marcus says, "you and your pops have spent a lot of time thinking about this."

"Yeah," I say sinking the ten, nine and twelve, "the funny thing though is that while my father and I are very cognizant of the need to concentrate on each and every shot, we inevitably fail to do so when we shoot stick together. In fact, instead of concentrating we tend to do everything but. We catch up on things, talk about other people we play with, and dissect every topic under the lights, including the need to concentrate. Invariably though, the actual act of concentrating on the game before us tends to get lost."

"Yeah, but do you guys really care who wins?"

"That's funny too, because at its most pure, the Tony moment is not just about seizing opportunities, but about entering into a whole new relationship with the world around you as well, something you could argue my father and I accomplish through the mere act of shooting pool. It's not like we had always played pool and it's not like we've always spent that kind of time together. Pool actually allows us to relate in a whole new way."

"Sort of like us, we work together, but we barely talk, right?"

"Sure," I say sinking the eleven and the fifteen.

"I think that dudes need something to relate over, like competition, or at least the idea of competition. Males need to do male stuff, otherwise it is all too conscious and shit."

"Exactly," I say sinking the thirteen, "pool was his game, not mine, but, when I started playing a few years ago, I realized that I had found my hook. Pool is not just common ground. It's like a neutral and almost parallel universe kind of ground. Once at the table we can talk about the game or life or not talk at all, because unlike everything else when you're shooting stick, if you need to stop and shoot, you do and no one questions it. It's not like people expect to talk during games."

I line-up the thirteen and try not to focus on the fourteen lingering just off the left or the eight ball which is nicely positioned in the center of the table.

I miss, just barely, but I miss.

Marcus walks up to the table and doesn't say a word.

"Are you sure we can't call it the Marcus moment?" he says minutes later after he runs the table.

45.

It's Thursday and Thursday is support group day at work. We have a group of five to six clients who meet once a week to talk about their meds, their benefits, and how things are going. I am the co-leader of the group with Marcus.

The group is small today. There is Rhoda and Jessie, Larry and this other very angry junkie guy James. I haven't seen Jessie since the encounter on the "L" tracks months before and I had almost forgotten about it.

Almost.

We always start with a group check-in. We go around the circle, and one by one the participants are expected to share what's happening in their lives at that very moment.

Rhoda goes first.

"I am really happy this week. I spoke to my mom and she's going to help me find my daughter. She says she doesn't really remember her or when she was removed, but we weren't in contact for awhile and so she says she might be wrong and that she can help me when my meds are stabilized. Yes, I decided to start taking them again. I didn't want to, but I want my old life back. I'm also going to go have dinner at home, which I haven't done in a long time because of my government intelligence work and so I'm excited about that. Jessie's coming with me, and that makes me really happy, because he makes me happy, having someone in my life, someone there for me. Well, it makes a difference. Life is hard, and wonderful. And so I'm happy this week."

"Well, I'm happy too," Jessie says, "and sure, it will be nice to meet your mom, though, I know you're up to something, and I know you're running around behind my back…"

"I'm not Jessie, it's not true."

"Yeah, well what about Clark Kent over there?" Jessie responds motioning to me.

"No, Jessie, no I haven't even sat by him in months. We haven't even been here."

"Yeah, well I'm watching, always watching."

"Hey, Larry," Marcus interjects, "do you have anything that you want to share?"

"No thank you, I got nothing. I'm kind of shaky from my meds this week and feeling kind of slow, but no nothing. And you, do you have anything, you're next?"

As co-leaders Marcus and I are supposed to take a turn as well.

"No," Marcus responds, "I don't have anything. James?"

"Well, I already had dinner with my family this week. As it turns out, my dad wasn't drunk all the time when we were kids. He wanted to be sure I know that in case there was any confusion. He also wanted to be sure that I knew that he didn't scream and stomp around the house either. Oh, and that my sister and I are fucked-up junkies just because, well, who knows, because my parents, they have nothing to do with this, any of this. It's a big fucking mess, but it's not on them, no, fuck no. And fuck them. Hey, you got anything?" he asks me turning to me.

I am not comfortable with checking-in and it's not that I have a general aversion to sharing, I don't think, it's that these are people with real problems, mental illness and homelessness, substance abuse and violence, and not only do I know little about what it is they're experiencing, but I am embarrassed to compare my ridiculous and petty concerns with theirs.

"Yeah, no, not a lot, things are mellow, work and home, go running. I'm cool," I say as I usually do.

"Bullshit," James screams, "I don't believe a word of that. Things are not mellow, things are never mellow and you motherfucker need to start getting down into the muck with us. C'mon man, this is bullshit, seriously, be real, what the fuck!"

"Hey, why didn't you yell at Marcus, he didn't say anything either?"

"Fuck him dude, I'm talking to you, you're my fucking project. Now give us something motherfucker."

Where did this come from? Yes, I am lying, and I am telling stories, but I didn't realize it was so obvious.

"All right, fine, fuck it. You want to know what's going on. You want to know how my dad is dying from this really fucked-up form of cancer and how doctors can keep promising they know how to save him, but they don't and they can't and so he will be dead soon and I'm not sure how to deal with that? Or how about the fact that my dad wasn't always living with us when I was kid and I'm sure I have a lot of unresolved shit related to that, but I just don't know how to square that with my dad being so sick it seems all wrong to start discussing this now? I know you would probably also like to know that I've been drinking a lot, especially when I'm home, and when I'm out drinking I sometimes sleep with women other than my wife, including one who once followed me home when I was a kid, so I know there's some twisted and safe nostalgia-laden element to all this though I just can't say for sure, because again, I'm mellow and everything is cool."

Everyone looks stunned.

"So, how was that?" I ask.

"That's all we were asking for," James replies. "It feels good to know that normal people have problems too."

46.

Oh therapist of little hands and curly hair, you have never pushed me like James the junkie has, and yet here I am looking at you across the room as I knead my thighs with my fingers and wonder whether I am prohibited from punching James in the face when next I see him. He has made me feel things and express them, and it is infuriating. He has also made me think about my father, which would feel even more wrong if it wasn't so fucking helpful and illuminating.

I have told you all about my father haven't I, I must have, right, especially since you sit there looking at me knowingly, like you knew we'd get here, that this was a plan of yours, and that maybe I've been hiding my real feelings from you, that maybe there is some rage in the mix, which I could potentially talk about with you now.

What will work for you though, what's right? How about this?

"There was my father leaving home, only to come home again, and yet somehow I just don't think I ever let myself try and understand how crazy it all was. I also don't think I understood how in the midst of all the confusion and imbalance I tried to create some stability and construct a world of my own making, where balance and cool and a sense of calm ruled the day, regardless of what was happening at night. It's funny really because it wasn't so hard to do. And it isn't to this day. I can reel in my emotions and feel nothing if needed. I can also do my best to protect others from harm even as I felt so little protection myself. I can even fake my way through the day pretty well, with jokes and smiles and storytelling, and the impression that all is good in the world. Well, I could, before James."

"So, James confronting you was helpful," the therapist says. "Maybe you need to be confronted to feel things. Is that possible?"

"Sure," I squeak, barely loud enough to be heard.

"And how does that make you feel?"

I pause. How much of me does she want?

"You know," I say, "maintaining a semblance of control takes a lot of effort because it has always greatly depended on me not just believing in my own my thinking, but always working to ensure that nothing ever put a dent in my armor, which was all good and well until I got angry, or sad, or wished I could cause someone pain, but wouldn't allow myself to feel any of that because I could not and would not allow myself to feel weak for even a second."

"Which is a big deal to you, isn't it?" she says.

"I suppose nothing is bigger to me," I reply, "my father never let those walls down or us in, not entirely anyway, which left me in a funky, confused place where I defined my emotions whether that was sadness, confusion, insecurity, embarrassment and anger as signs of weakness. And maybe I have the chance to have a better handle on all that now, but do I know any better why people leave, or maybe more importantly why he left? I don't think so, not really anyway, and that's fucked up really in so may ways, not the least of which is recognizing for the first time that when he left home he was leaving me as well."

"We can build on that," the therapist says.

47.

I'm not sure if it occurs to me when I am out running, lingering one night in front of the bathroom mirror or languishing in Thirsty's, but somewhere and at some point I decide that writing is something I need to do. Not something I might enjoy or that might be cool, though these are possibilities, but something I must do. I have always kept a journal, and I was already journaling about what was going on with my dad and his illness with the idea that these notes could be something bigger somehow, but suddenly I am writing about the act of writing, day after day, wondering how to start, and when I will start, but recognizing that I have no idea how that works or how someone even begins to figure it out.

And then something magical happens. Kerri and I go to a party and when I throw our coats on the bed in the guest room I see *Zen in the Art of Writing* by Ray Bradbury on the bookshelf. I take the slim volume off of the shelf, sit down on the bed, begin to read and keep reading until Kerri walks in and reminds me that we are at a party and I am supposed to be socializing. I stop reading then, but what sticks me with me is the suggestion that writers should create a list of possible story ideas and then when they want to write they should scan that list and see what sticks.

I start making lists. On the train. On planes. During concerts. I start connecting ideas that seem to hang together. And then I start fleshing out these ideas, adding conflicts and characters, always scribbling, on napkins, in notebooks, on pages from the *New Yorker*. I also realize that I always wanted my journaling to lead to something more, and that I was always writing myself notes about potential story ideas that have slowly been collecting in my head and stacking up like planes circling an airport and hoping to land.

At first though, I do not connect any of this sudden sense of urgency to my father or the fact that he has been a writer and illustrator or even that he is dying and that maybe I am trying to make some connection.

I do think about the movie *American Pop*, however, and about how one generation of males in this family after another wants to be a musician, and not just a musician, but a star, and yet each falls short until the son of the son of the son hits it big.

I also think about my father, his father before him and their respective frustrations about art and education and being someone. I realize then that I want to be that guy in *American Pop* who transcends the father, and if I'm going to do this I need to start writing.

48.

I'm not talking. But I don't think this is because I'm upset or discouraged or lost in some never-ending, *Groundhogs Day*, cycle of negative thoughts.

I think I am not talking because I am enjoying the light breeze wafting over my face and the sound of the waves lapping onto the shore at my feet.

I might even be not talking because of the seven or eight beers I have slowly consumed as we have sat here in our beach chairs.

Maybe I am just not talking, because I'm just not talking and sometimes people do that. That would be nice anyway.

"Is this weird for you?" Kerri asks.

I do not respond immediately.

"It must be, it's weird for me," Kerri says.

She then reaches over and squeezes my hand.

Every spring the extended family gathers at this little house my parents own in Sandwich out on Cape Cod. Some stay, some just come and go, and we do this because one time my mom suggested we do so because we never see each other as a group any more. We do this because it is the one time of year the whole family gets together. We do this because it is a wonderful gathering/happening/ritualistic family event that we do, and will do, again, and again, with little change, because, like Thanksgiving, it is what it is, a chance to break bread, celebrate family and tell the same stories.

Of course, there have been, and will be, changes or alterations along the way. For example, this is the first time we didn't rent *Short Cuts* and watch it together, all of us, crammed into the living room. At first we didn't notice this, but then we did, and someone asked why. No one needs to see *Short Cuts* again, but the first year we met here, we all saw it in the theater, driving like mad through the rain to get there, running in just as the previews were ending, and so every year we watch it.

Not this year though, and when we realized this, it took us a moment to figure out why this was.

It was my mother that had insisted we could get to *Short Cuts* that night. It had been raining all day and we had been stuck in the house and she had insisted we get out. She had willed us to be there on time and she is the one who rents the movie every year, part nostalgia, part triumph, we had doubted her, said we couldn't get there, and we had been wrong.

But my mom's not here. In fact, we are missing my mom and dad. The doctor said no to the travel and to being around so many people in such cramped quarters. He also questioned my father's ability to fill his ever-growing need for transfusions while on the road.

As people have come and gone this weekend they have certainly asked about my dad and how he was doing, commenting on how it is too bad that he wasn't allowed to come. But this didn't happen a lot, or as much as I might have guessed. And maybe this has to do with people not wanting me to have to dwell on it. Or maybe it's that they themselves do not want to dwell on what's happening, the reality being all too bleak whether they are immersed in it a lot like we are or just a little like most everybody else.

The thing is I imagine this is what it will be like eventually, there will be the Sandwich gathering, no dad to attend it and so we'll just have to adjust the model. We'll get there, and we will think about him, and it will suck, and it will seem wrong, and lacking, but it, like life, will continue to happen on some level. And there will be times, like this weekend, that we will notice his loss a lot, and other times it will just be a little, and then other times not at all.

All that said, I can only take so much change and so much insight at one time, especially after seven or eight beers.

I squeeze Kerri's hand.

"Hey," I say "I'm too drunk to drive, would you mind taking me to the video store?"

49.

I'm dreaming about babies. It's true. Now it wasn't much of a dream mind you, or at least I don't remember much about it. But there was this baby, tiny, ours, and he, definitely a he, was in a crib, and I just wasn't sure how he got there. I kept walking out of the room and back in, assuming he wouldn't be there the next time, but he was, every time I went in. I finally stood there for a moment trying to figure out how and when this transpired, but I couldn't, it didn't make sense and I had no idea where he came from. Eventually, I just picked him up, walked down the hall and yelled out to Kerri, "Did we forget to tell my parents that we had a baby?"

I don't know exactly what that means, nor can I say why the first thought that came to me was wondering whether we had told my parents or not.

Still, what I do know is that we've been talking babies lately, and it's disconcerting really, because what has begun to haunt me most about my dad's illness is that it seems likely that he will never meet our kids. He's not doing worse or anything. He's not doing better either, but he's not doing worse, he has stopped doing worse, which was definitely where we were heading not so long ago.

But, what if he continues not doing worse, not better, but not worse, is that possible? It could be and so I have to wonder about the new drugs he's been taking at Johns Hopkins. I know these new drugs aren't supposed to kick-in until the third month, and that we're only in the second.

I also know that he can take them for six months, and so we really don't know what they are capable of.

I also know that we are not supposed to get our hopes up with this disease, especially when nothing else has worked and there's nothing else they can really do for him. But knowing something and wanting something are vastly different things and so I am going to get my hopes up, if only a little, and I am going to let myself believe that while he might not be around forever and ever like my grandfather, he might just be around long enough to meet that kid I dreamt about and that Kerri and I have been talking about maybe having.

Because we may not have thought we could have a child with the hope that it might save my dad's life, but that doesn't mean it didn't get us thinking about children or wondering when we should have one. And if we're going to wonder, than why not wonder if my father could be around to meet said kid?

50.

It is late, I am frazzled and I am running far up into the hills behind my parent's house. I did not plan to come in this weekend. Things were okay, fine, not worse, and I was dreaming, but now I am running and trying to get away from the thoughts that have been haunting me all day as I called Southwest, got on the train, ran through the airport, flew into some small town and its small airport, got into a car and drove home, again, never stopping to breathe, never doing an inventory of the thoughts swirling, endlessly swirling in my head and never even stopping to talk to anyone, just getting home, strapping on my running shoes and going back out, trying to breathe and trying to think. One step. Then another. Breathe. Pump arms. Step. Step. Breathe. Lean into the hill. Breathe. Step. Relax. Relax. Breathe. And back home again, calmer and able to talk.

When I walk into the house I see my mom sitting at the dining room table and drinking coffee. She is staring out the back window.

"Hey mom."

Nothing.

"Mom!"

"Yes?" she says turning around and looking at me.

The thing to do here is to be soft, and gentle, not focus so much on myself and ask her how she's doing. I can do that.

"Okay, so what am I supposed to think and how am I supposed to feel? Because I am feeling very distressed right now, and no, I'm not all that surprised I guess, but what's going on exactly?" I ask her proceeding to focus on myself and not ask her how she's doing, much less be soft or gentle.

"Dad went back into the hospital last night," she says, "he had a fever and what appeared to be a staph infection. He does not have a staph infection, but he does have atypical pneumonia."

"And? What?"

"It's not critical or anything, yet, but he's got it, and he shouldn't really have visitors, and who knows if they can beat it back."

"What about this cell count?" I ask. "Are they getting worse too?"

"No," she says, "his counts are not getting any worse, but his immune system is breaking down."

We were warned about this, that these kinds of opportunistic diseases could strike at any time regardless of how he was feeling or how he was doing, but we ignored this, we were dreaming about other things, and so it's really scary now that it's happening, certainly scarier than counts dropping. It feels more real and concrete, because the cell counts always seemed so high and dropped so incrementally it felt like they could do so forever, pneumonia though can just kill him, just like that.

Of course even as I'm thinking this, I wonder whether I am truly allowing myself to consider the possibility that we are going to lose him. Really lose him. Because even while it is hard to believe that he might actually be saved at this moment it's not so clear to me that I have ever truly believed he won't be, not today, not ever. So, I have to ask whether I am truly aware of what's really going on and if I'm not, how do I get more aware and how will I know when I am?

I don't know the answer to this, and so instead of trying to figure it out, I just go and hug my mom instead. I want to be selfless and caring, because she deserves that, especially when my only other option is confusion.

51.

Lawn girl is sitting on the floor of her room and slowly rocking back and forth, her arms wrapped around her knees which are pulled-up to her chest. She is staring off into space. She is no longer crying.

The morning light is cutting through her bedroom window and her long honey streaked hair is glowing. She looks beautiful. She looks over at me, her face full of rage and pain.

"Get out," she says, "please, just get the fuck out and don't come back, ever."

I start to say something, but she puts her hand-up and waves me off.

Maybe it's best to rewind at this point. I got home and I was spinning. I ran and felt calmer. I spoke to my mom and eventually I felt okay, okay enough. Still, I was feeling aimless, so I put on the television and began channel surfing. SportsCenter. Tony Robbins. QVC. Mindless all of it. And perfect. But then I stumbled into TNT and there it was, *Running on Empty*, and as I watched River Phoenix saying goodbye to his parents, knowing that he might never see them again, I started getting choked-up. I don't want to be choked-up though and I don't want to cry, can't cry.

I turned off the television and headed out into the night. I meandered through the streets, past the GIANT supermarket and muffler shop where Pudgie's Pizza was when we were kids, and then the AM/PM and Garrett's Hardware store, through the parking lot next to CVS and into Thirsty's.

I grabbed a spot at the end of the bar and ordered a Yuengling, and then another, and she was there, lawn girl, Jessie, smiling and dancing around and lovely, but I know it's time, time to ignore her, time to be faithful, and time to let her know that whatever it is we have been up to, and whether there may or may not be strings attached, I'm all through with it, I have a wonderful wife and I've been acting out, drawn to her and to the cheating by a pull I don't entirely get. And I think she'll understand this, because we're cool, and she's cool. After three more beers the reasons behind this speech aren't as clear to me though, and as I start to kiss her back at her apartment, I really want to believe it isn't a big deal, but then I open my eyes, and she opens hers, and there's a look, an intensity that scares me and I pull back. This is a mistake, a terrible mistake and this thing is definitely a big deal to her.

"What?" she says.

"Uh."

"What? C'mon, you can say it."

"I'm not sure this is right," I say, "I don't think I can do this anymore."

She doesn't speak at first.

"You're the guy I've been looking for," she says with an urgency that surprises me, "and you're the guy I was always looking for. I measure everyone against the idea of you."

What?

I try to speak.

"No," she says, "don't say anything, I know I just sounded crazy, but I don't care. Can we just get back to what we're doing? Please."

"No."

"We have something here," she says, "and you can't deny that. And I've helped you. I've helped you."

She's growing more intense and I'm scared. I don't know how I am supposed to get out of this.

"You have helped me," I say, "and I appreciate it, but it's done now."

"You're a user," she says, "and a jerk, and fuck you if you think you are leaving here tonight."

I don't know what to do or say. I'm desperate.

"You liked my father, didn't you, and not just liked him," I suddenly blurt out.

Where did that came from?

She gets up. She walks around the room. She's crying. She sits down on the floor.

"That's not true," she finally says, "but even if I had, so what, he wasn't a prick like you."

And then for a long time we sit there, me on her bed, and her on the floor, rocking back and forth. She is staring off into space. She is no longer crying.

The morning light is cutting through her bedroom window and her long honey streaked hair is glowing. She looks beautiful.

And I fully realize for the first time that I am here and with her, not because of nostalgia, but because of her connection to my dad, however tenuous or warped it may be.

She looks over at me, her face full of rage and pain.

"Get out," she says, "please, just get the fuck out and don't come back, ever."

I start to say something, but she puts her hand-up and waves me off.

And I leave.

52.

Father's Day again and one year since we flew home following the diagnosis. My father is back on the chemotherapy protocol; still receiving transfusions, though not quite so often; and I really don't quite know what to say about all that.

What I can say is that Tiger Woods ran off with the U.S. Open by 15 strokes. The Yankees got shelled. There are rumors about Patrick Ewing being traded to the Wizards for Juwan Howard. There are calls for the police to boycott Bruce Springsteen and new leadership in Syria. There's not much to say about the Dow, nor the presidential race for that matter. Jacob Lawrence is dead and Prince William turns 18 any day now.

Last night Kerri and I saw the documentary *Pop and Me*, the story of a father and son who traveled the world for six months and interviewed fathers and sons throughout the journey. As I watched it I thought about my dad and how we will likely never have the chance to do something like that, travel together in such a fashion, or make a movie together or whatever that thing is we never got to do.

I also thought about how Kerri and I may have a son some day and if we do, maybe we will have to do some of the things my dad and I never did.

I suppose I could have discussed this with Kerri, but somehow it got me thinking about my mom and how she would want to talk about something like this.

I call my mom.

"Hey," I say, "how's he doing?"

"Tired, fighting, tired."

"You sound tired," I say.

"No, well, maybe a little, it's all right. How are you, what are you guys up to."

"We saw this movie that made me think about dad."

"What?"

"It was called *Pop and Me*, it was a documentary about a father and son and how they traveled the world interviewing fathers and sons. They also got to talk about their own relationship."

"How did that make you feel?"

"How did it make me feel, like we're not going to be able to do any of that."

"Any of what?"

"I don't know, I guess I'm talking about travel and projects and who knows what on the one hand, but on the other I'm talking about finding a way to communicate, letting someone, dad, in on what I'm experiencing whether that's pain, anger or sadness."

"You could try to talk to him."

"Maybe, but I have to admit, even as I think about dad, I'm also thinking about the kids Kerri and I haven't had yet, and how if we have a son, I don't know whether we will we be able to connect in some deep and meaningful way."

"Of course you will," she says, "your father and you were very close when you were little. He was great. Maybe things got confused along the way, but he was great and he was always there for you, and you can be like that too."

"I guess I just have a lot of work to do and I don't know whether I can do it. I also don't know when I got so cheesy. Can you please tell me to shut the fuck up the next time I start talking like this."

"I think that's a job for one of your friends."

"Good enough, thanks mom."

"Goodnight honey."

And I am feeling cheesy, terribly so, but I am willing to do the work. Imagine all of the things my boy and I will do.

We will watch football as we lay around on Sunday afternoons, buried under the New York Times and a pile of pillows. We will wrestle, for sure, endlessly, poking, prodding, tickling and elbowing.

We will walk across the Grand Canyon together crossing from the North Rim to the South or maybe it's from the South to the North, I don't know which, I just know I want us to end up at the lodge, beds, steaks, and beer awaiting our arrival.

We may very well make movies and write together too. And we will definitely shoot pool of course, anywhere and everywhere, in dark and smoky rooms, with beat up tables and cigarette scarred rugs. And we'll run, long into the night and year-round, not a care in the world, but the next step, and then the one after that.

Or maybe we will do none of this, but that will be okay, because we will be able to talk, our defenses down, our need to connect greater than any of the pain we have inflicted on one another. Of course, there is no kid yet, but there may be one someday and I need to get ready for that.

53.

Smack.

Huh?

Something has hit me in the face.

It's my book.

It's late and Kerri and I are in bed reading and looking to wind down. I am on my back and gripping the cover of *Cruddy* in each hand as it lightly bounces on my chest with each shallow breath and Kerri is lying on her stomach and leaning over *She Comes Undone* which lies flat on the bed just inches below her face.

I now notice that I have been struggling to keep my eyes open and that I have gone from alert and engaged to half-awake and dozing with no notice at all. I force my eyes to re-open and start reading.

Smack.

Cruddy has fallen onto my face as I drifted off again.

Kerri looks over at me and says, "That's it, bedtime for you."

She leans over to turn off the lights when the phone rings. Who would call this time of night? I assume it must be my mom. It can't be good.

"Hello," Kerri says.

"What, slow down," she says.

I cannot make out who she's talking to.

"Is that my mom?" I whisper, now fully awake.

"What about the baby?" Kerri asks the mystery caller even as she turns away from me and sits up in bed.

"Okay," she says, "call me if you want to talk some more, any time, tonight, tomorrow, whenever."

"And, take care of yourself, all right, I love you."

Kerri hangs up the phone and starts to cry.

"What happened," I ask, "who was that, what's going on?"

"Slow down," she says wiping away her tears with the back of her hands, first the right, then the left.

I wait until she's ready.

Kerri walks out of our room and into the bathroom. She runs the water and washes her face. She stares into the mirror. And then she comes back.

"That was Amy," she says.

Amy is her old college roommate. She's very hot and was once prone to ripping off her shirt after getting drunk in bars. Sadly, she doesn't do that as much anymore.

"She's thinking of leaving Steve."

Steve is the husband. He's a tool. Well, he's a nice guy, she just happened to marry her father that's all.

"She's not happy and she doesn't even know why, she just knows she can't live with Steve any more, even if that means leaving Eve behind."

Eve is their baby. Eve is very cute. How could anyone leave Eve anywhere?

"Can we agree that if we ever have a child and then one of us wants to leave we will have to take the child with us, none of that *Kramer vs. Kramer* bullshit for us?"

I say this trying to sound funny, I fail miserably.

"That's not funny," Kerri says, "she feels like she's dying inside. It's terrible. She's sitting in her car in the driveway with a suitcase next to her and Steve doesn't even know she's outside."

"I'm sorry," I say, "I was trying to lighten the mood

I give her a hug and she puts her head on my shoulder. I slowly rock back and forth and eventually she falls asleep.

54.

I cannot fall asleep though. I am apparently more upset by Amy's call than I realized. Kerri and I just don't know anyone else in any failed marriages. How's this possible? Are they all in good marriages? Maybe, but how good is our marriage? I've never thought about this and I don't know how Kerri feels about it, because I've never talked about it with her. Would one of us ever leave? Would we know how too? Why would we want to?

There is, was, lawn girl of course, but I never thought of that whole thing as akin to wanting to leave Kerri, it was more like running, an escape, a place to go where all the day to day and moment to moment stuff melted away.

It's the first time I grasp that Kerri might want to leave me for something like that and I feel sick. It's also the first time that I realize that I might want to leave her someday. Or that I could even want to now, though I don't think I want to, nor have any idea why I would.

Am I happy? Do I even know? It's so easy to just be in things, living, and doing, without thinking. But is it even my leaving that I'm thinking about or the idea that people leave, can leave, will leave, and maybe not even know why or be able to explain it, because they don't know themselves, and what they know they cannot communicate or be honest about, because honesty sucks, it's painful and hurts people, and why would anyone consciously want to do that? They wouldn't. Would they?

Which makes me think about my dad, why he left when he did, whether he ever knew why he was doing what he was doing and how little any of that was discussed.

And now I'm spinning, the thoughts ping-ponging through my head, faster and faster, all warp speed, harder and harder to track or understand.

Historically this is when I would run. I would head out and after awhile I would have some kind insight, some calm, and it would be okay for the moment, the shadows held at bay for one more night.

But tonight is different because tonight I want to write about all of the confusion, fear and sadness running through my head, even though I've yet to start writing and have no true sense of what that means.

There are my lists though all full of story ideas and their various permutations. And there is one story that is jumping out at me, maybe the only story I could have ever started with. It is a story that ties together the different experiences I had with people I knew as a kid who had left their wives in one form or another. There is my hockey playing neighbor's dad for example. But really, ultimately, it is a story that explores my father in particular. And me.

It will be written from the perspective of a child who cannot make sense of why people leave and ultimately leaves his wife as an adult, still confused about the dynamics and reasons that underlie such decisions.

I can visualize the words and I can see how the story is going to evolve. The characters are vibrant and real to me. Their dialogue is clear. And the piece is being written in my head even as stare at the blank pages before me, unmoving, pen in hand.

I know now that I just need to start.

And so I do.

55.

"How are you doing?" the therapist asks.

I try not to look at her hands, wanting to be less fixated and compulsive, but I fail, my compulsions are a constant, as much a part of my day as waking-up or brushing my teeth.

"How am I doing," I say, "I could talk about something that has been weighing on me."

"Please do."

"Okay, but it's not my sense that my father's inclusion in the Johns Hopkins' protocol he just entered appears to be ever more short-lived because of some bullshit about how what the doctors there are seeking is a dramatic improvement, because achieving any kind stability thirteen months into this nightmare is far from what they are looking for, regardless mind you of just how amazing that is for all the rest of us."

"What's going on," she says looking right at me with her kind eyes, "I'm not sure I follow?"

"They say they don't know what the side effects of the protocol are, so why risk more problems for my father down the road, as if there's definitely a down the road or something."

"Okay."

"Because this of course isn't all about making sure the drug company money continues to come in by ensuring that data that merely shows stability is not available for review,"

I say getting worked-up. "The doctors would never think of pulling something like that, would they?"

"You're upset. This must be hard news to hear."

I almost start to cry, almost, but I right myself.

"You know," I say, "it's not like I'm really thinking about any of this anyway, well, I am, obviously, but at the moment what I'm really thinking about is depression, and how my dad definitely seems depressed, his mood feeling like depression, his tears looking like depression and his dreams sounding like depression."

"Okay, so you don't want to talk about the protocol?" she says.

I can't. I won't. It's too intense and I want to be pragmatic, stoic.

"No, I'm cool, and I'm done with that, what I'm thinking about though is Kubler-Ross' five stages of dying, because depression is the fourth stage, the first three being denial, anger and bargaining, with acceptance the fifth and final stage, right?"

"Right."

"And you may be thinking about why I'm thinking so much about this," I say, "but if acceptance is the next stage, maybe it will bring him some peace you know."

"It could," she says, "but it might not be quite that linear."

"Okay, sure," I say, "and you know I could also be thinking about this, because if we are, or were, this close to the final stage, maybe it also says something about how close we are to the end, what that means, why this happens and what comes next."

"It might," she says.

It might?

I decide then and there that I am going to need to take a break from seeing the therapist until after all of this is over with. I can't talk about the possibilities anymore, how they may, or may not, play out and how they may, or may not, make me feel.

If I am going to spend any more time exploring any of this, it is going to need to be based in reality, and this is definitely not reality, not yet anyway.

I look at her lovely hands one more time and then head out and into the day.

56.

It's funny how things work though, because even as I decide to pull back from therapy, I am writing more and more all the time, it's my new outlet, and my new compulsion, and I'm all in.

What's also funny, however, is that I can't wait to show my first story to Kerri and my mom and dad. And despite the fact that it is about a husband leaving his wife even as he reflects on his own father leaving his family, it never occurs to me that it might engender some anxiety for Kerri or any pain for my parents, specifically my dad, whose presence, or lack thereof looms so large in the story.

Maybe I needn't have worried about these things though, because it is a piece everyone in the family really likes, especially my dad, which only gets me spinning even more, and writing every day, the backlog of stories that have accumulated on my lists waiting there for me like planes lined-up on the tarmac and ready for flight.

When a friend of mine asks me to read something at this gallery opening, I suddenly have a number of things to choose from, but I select this first piece, it is my initial foray into the world of writing and without it, there would be nothing else to choose from.

I ask Kerri to videotape the reading so I can show it to my parents during our next visit and my dad and I end up watching the tape together by ourselves.

As we watch it he starts to cry.

"Hey dad," I ask, "do you want me to stop the tape?"

"No, I want to watch it," he replies.

I leave it on, but he continues to cry. We don't talk much while watching the tape and I can't even look at him because it's just too painful.

"I feel so bad about the decisions I made and the affect it had on all of us," he says when it's over.

And then he cries some more.

"Dad, it's all right, it was a long time ago," I say trying to comfort him, but it doesn't do the trick, not really.

I am struck of course by the mere fact that my dad is even crying, but I am also struck once again by the fact that once again it hasn't occurred to me that my dad might find the story at least somewhat upsetting.

I wonder what it says about me. I also wonder how passive-aggressive and cruel the whole act has been from the start and how whether it's possible that I am angry at him for all that once went down, but was never really discussed.

I then decide to ignore this and give him a hug instead.

57.

We've been having some drinks after work and as I step out of The Green Mill, I throw on my Walkman and walk up to the train platform. Once there, I start to read the newspaper and quickly lose myself in Bruce.

"I awoke and I imagined the hard things that pulled us apart Will never again, sir, tear us from each other's hearts—I got dressed, and to that house I did ride from out on the road, I could see—its windows shining in light—I walked up the steps and stood on the porch a woman I didn't recognize came and spoke to me through a chained door—I told her my story, and who I'd come for She said 'I'm sorry, son, but no one by that name lives here anymore'—My father's house shines hard and bright it stands like a beacon calling me in the night—Calling and calling, so cold and alone—Shining cross this dark highway where our sins lie unatoned."

"Hey you, over here, right here, look at me."

Huh?

"I said look at me."

I have been so lost in the music and reading, I have not been paying attention to the homeless guy coming out of the shadows and now standing right in front of me, maybe an arm's length away.

"What's up motherfucker," Jessie says all tense and coiled, "we have unfinished business."

Ah, shit.

My immediate reaction is to run and there's nothing wrong with that. It's safe, even smart. My second reaction is to kick him in the balls. Less safe and I can already feel the stress creeping up my back, the muscles starting to knot and unknot.

But then I think about how Marcus handled things with Trina and about my dad. How my dad isn't going to be around much longer, how he won't get to fix any of the things he regrets and how I don't want to feel like that. And so maybe there's a third way things can go down here, and if there is, if that's real, I need to go that way.

"No, there's no unfinished business here," I reply in the firmest, calmest voice I can, my eyes locked on his. "I'm telling you that there's nothing going on with Rhoda and there isn't going to be. I have a wife and I love her. I also have a job and I have to see your girlfriend on that job, but that's it, and I need you to get good with that."

I have tried to stay strong. I have tried to be honest and forthright. I have tried to confront Jessie as an adult. And I have tried not to be scared.

"There's nothing going on," Jessie's says visibly relaxing, "and there won't be. That's what you're saying?"

I take a deep breath. I try to relax as well.

"That's what I'm saying."

"And that's all I need to hear then. Just tell the truth and talk to me like a man. Is that so tough?"

"I guess not."

He reaches out his hand to shake. I pause.

"Relax motherfucker," he says.

Relax motherfucker. I can do that. I take a breath.

We shake. He walks away. And I stand there until the adrenaline stops coursing through my veins and I'm not shaking so much.

58.

After I get on the train and get home, I lace up my running shoes and head right out into the night. The Jessie thing went well. I should be proud. I am proud.

I think about my dad and how he would have handled it. They might have fought. But would they have talked? It's funny really being out here, running, and thinking about my dad, because my dad may have come and gone at times, but I always told myself that nothing had changed, and it had no affect on me.

I just didn't feel anything. And I kept telling myself this, despite the alcohol and the drugs and sleepless nights. I just ran and ran, fueled by the electricity crackling in the night, I would step into the darkness as I have tonight and I would run until I had felt everything I could not during the day, dancing home beneath the glittering stars, arms raised Rocky-like in victory.

There was no destination those nights, nor was there a plan. No, running was about escape, and escape I did, step by step, mile by mile. And over the years I just kept going, I had no choice, I had nothing else, no other tools, no where to turn. Running became who I am and what I do and I never thought much about it beyond that, didn't want to really.

Now though, what I want is to find a place where I can let I myself feel the pain, frustration, and anger that I cannot face otherwise. And running lets me do that too. Running has always allowed me to maintain a sense of control in a world that I felt constantly conspired against me. It also let me somehow believe I could still do anything even as every other moment during the day made me feel otherwise.

Until tonight, because it is only tonight that all of this makes sense to me, and it is only tonight that I realize that I am capable of so much more.

59.

My father has been bounced from his protocol at Johns Hopkins for remaining stable. Stable. Not getting better, but not getting worse either. Stable. Check that, he was stable.

I call Jerry.

"He got bounced" I say.

"I know," Jerry says, "I spoke to mom."

"It blows," I say, "it's fucking terrible."

"I know," he says.

He's so mellow, it's creepy and it makes me think that I made this call for me, that he doesn't need to talk about it, only I do, which then makes me feel selfish, but that doesn't make me stop, no, can't stop, won't stop.

"He was stable," I continue.

"Yeah," he says, "I saw him right after you did."

"His peripheral blast counts...," I start to say.

"What are those again?" he asks.

"They're the exploding premature blood cells...," I respond.

"Right"

"Yeah, well, they're so expansive they can now be seen outside the blood itself."

"He looks really emaciated," Jerry says.

"And tired," I say.

"And let's not forget that lingering cough," Jerry says no longer sounding quite so chill, "I don't know why that fucking cough bothers me so much, but it sounds like death, you know?"

"I know man, I do," I say, "and maybe these changes have nothing to do with being dropped from the protocol, but I do wonder, and when I don't wonder, I think about how comfortable I kind of started feeling again. Not confident of course, but somewhat comfortable for sure, because stable isn't bad, and who knows where stable could have lead, and just how long he even needs to live until they find something even better. You can't ever truly gain any real comfort though. I can try to convince myself that there is hope because one positive thing or another seems to be happening at some particular moment, but doing so is always a mistake."

"Dad says that maybe it would be easier for all of us if this just ended," Jerry says. "And what am I supposed to say to that, no, it wouldn't? Because that's what I say, it's what I have to say, I want him for as long as I can have him."

"Life would be easier though," I say, "wouldn't it, not better, but easier."

"I don't know," Jerry says sniffling.

I do know, and while I wouldn't trade for it, or wish for it, I know it's true. I also know though that my dad has been bounced from this protocol so they can protect their numbers. Stable doesn't get increases in funding and stable is not ever going to be deemed a success, it doesn't work that way.

"Hey Jerry," I say suddenly, "I have to go, I need to do something, are you going to be alright?"

"Yeah, sure, of course, I'm glad you called, I guess," he says letting out a small laugh.

I get off of the phone. I send my dad's doctor an e-mail and I ask her if she can live with herself having released a sick man from a protocol because he was merely stable and is now not only rapidly deteriorating, but sure to die sooner than he had to.

"Is your funding worth that," I ask, "and how does it feel to have his blood on your hands?"

She writes me back.

They didn't know if he would remain stable and these are untested drugs. They don't know what the long-term side effects are and what if he got worse, how could they risk that?

She writes this like there's something worse than someone rapidly hurtling towards their death. Is she actually reading what she's writing?

And then as the kicker she adds, "Just so you know, my father just died and I know how you must be feeling."

She knows how I must be feeling? Doubtful, she doesn't have to deal with people like her. Still, I want to enjoy this. I want her to suffer as well. She's killed my dad, hasn't she? But I can't enjoy it, how can I wish this shit on anyone. I can't, it's too terrible.

I write her back and I tell her I'm sorry to hear about her loss.

60.

The whole world has gone crazy I guess.

Fujimori says he will step down in Peru and Milosevic is trying to figure out how not to do so in Yugoslavia. Bush has regained the lead over Gore. In Prague they are being forced to defend against globalization. The markets are all down for the year. And the Knicks have traded Patrick Ewing to Seattle.

And my dad has been hospitalized, which is why I am sitting quietly in the Park Diner with my mother, drinking coffee and staring out the window watching the Susquehanna River pass by, as it always does, day after day, doing its job, sometimes higher and sometimes lower, but always flowing, with little change and less drama.

"He is coming out some time this week," my mom says putting on a brave face, though I don't know whether it's for my benefit or hers.

"But for how long?" I ask.

His white blood cell count shot up to 64,000 last week, a fatal or near fatal level depending on who you speak to, though it has been reigned back in for now.

"I don't know," she says, "the blast counts are at one-hundred percent, I don't know how far they can be pushed back."

"So what's next?" I ask.

"I don't know," she says looking out the window.

I don't know how she does this day after day, its so much easier to jet in and out, be here, then not, consumed, but not. I have a chance to breathe, she never does.

"We're in a different place now, aren't we," I say

"I guess, but I try not to think about it like that," she says regaining some of her normal energy.

"What sort of timeframe do you think we are talking about here?" I ask.

"You know," my mom says, "I don't think like that either. We're going to save him, that's all."

I want to tell her that I am not remotely prepared for what's coming. Am I tired? Yes, very. Am I freaked? Definitely, beyond freaked whatever that is. Am I stressed? I am, especially when I actually stop to think about what's going on. But am I prepared in any way? No, no way, and I don't know that I can be. It's too scary and too sad, and frankly just too hard to imagine, much less fathom.

The thing is, I can go to the hospital and visit with my father and his chemo-burned tongue, ever-thinner face and ever increasing resemblance to his mother. I can talk regret, and illness, and I'm cool, focused and collected. I can even watch them load him with chemo, red blood cells, platelets and Benadryl and I'm down. But am I remotely ready? No. Are you ever? I don't know, but can I tell my mom this, no, definitely not, she's still in it, and I need to get back in it as well.

61.

Tonight I decide not to go out running or head to Thirsty's. Both have served me well during this time. They have allowed me to deal with the uncertainties of my dad's illness and at times make more cogent decisions that had previously escaped me. They have also allowed me to ignore the stuff I wanted to ignore when I thought I needed to.

Things are different now though, the chance of loss and heartbreak is higher and while I can still decide to pretend things are better, or will be, its not the truth, and will not be truth and so I can allow myself to miss things, or I can be in it, fully in it and part of whatever's to come.

There's no real question here of course, there may be nothing worse than facing death, but there's nothing worse than not facing it either.

I head down to the hospital, and though it may be late, no one sweats visiting hours on the cancer ward. It's quiet here at night and nothing like it is during the day, with its hustle and bustle and nurses endlessly running around the halls caring for the constant flow of patients on their last legs and drifting fitfully to wherever their final resting place may be.

Of course, it's not just about the hustle and bustle, the hospital at night is a weird mélange of light and dark and shadows and glare as well. The room lights are all off, except for the occasional reading lamp, flickering images from late night talk shows or the random blips of light emerging from the endless array of machines people find themselves hooked-up to in this stage of life, or death, depending on where they sit and how they define the view.

The hall lights are all on however and shockingly bright for a place where people are trying to sleep or die peacefully. When combined with the spotless white walls and floors, roaming the halls here at night is more like drifting through a space capsule than a place of sickness and death. Of course, they don't want you to actually think about death while you are here, it needs to be hidden away, behind curtains and closed doors, and masked by drugs and tubes, just out of sight and mind, something better left to imagination if considered at all.

It is something you come to embrace, or at least accept. It's what death looks like in modern times, clean, antiseptic and hushed. The craziness and pain is kept to a minimum. The shock of what the end of life really looks like is minimized. This is no return to nature. And it is not real. Not usually. But tonight is different.

Because when I get to my dad's room the lights are on. Both the door and curtain are open, and he is wide awake and shivering well-beyond what might seem normal, or safe, anywhere else. He is hugging himself with his toothpick thin arms and when his teeth are not chattering, he is coughing, a bone-shattering cough that leaves a spray of bloody phlegm on his lips with each involuntary spasms.

I hung-out with him earlier today and last night after sitting with my mom at the Park Diner. I had watched him not only take oxygen through nose clips and suck on an inhaler to expand his bronchial tunes, but suddenly look very much like a dying guy, when even last week he could still pass for a guy who was merely dying.

But that didn't compare to this. This looks like something other than dying. This looks like torture, like someone wrestling with demons, both real and psychological.

"Hey dad, what's up," I say, trying to sound strong and cool, all the while trying not to notice how bony his now non-existent ass looks every time his robe flutters open.

"H-h-h-i baby," he says grimacing, but trying to smile and look tough all at once, "my fever has been spiking and dropping, bouncing up and down and up again all night, but now its up, too up, and it won't come down, and so they have me on this special mat, its chilled, freezing actually, and I have to stay on it if my temperature is going to stop climbing."

That's when I notice the red mat he is lying on. It looks like a coaster.

"How long have you been on it?" I ask.

"A-a-a-n hour," he says suddenly bouncing off of the mat, before briefly curling into fetal position.

"Is there anything I can do?" I say.

"N-n-n o, you can sit here, you can talk to me and tell me what you've been up to," he responds closing his eyes and coughing.

And so I do. I talk and talk. I adjust his pillow and dab his lips. I sit there late into the night and until they remove the mat because it's not making a difference.

I continue to sit there as he mercifully falls asleep, his cough retreating, his heavy breath becoming lighter.

This may be but another blip, or bump, or temporary setback. He may yet go home and fight for another day. But as I sit there wanting to be hopeful and straightening his blanket, I have to ask myself if this is any way to live, or if it's even living.

62.

I am back in the hospital. My father is not shaking. And this is good. What is odd though is that someone has decided that he needs to see a cardiologist. Some test has been run and his heart doesn't sound right. I am struck that in some way this seems like overkill. Say there is something wrong with his heart, will they try and fix it, can they fix it and why would they fix it even if they could, aren't we in the end game now, what's the point?

Still, this is a hospital, and they fix things, or at least try to figure out if they can. It's what they do here. If a garage thinks you probably need to junk your car they will still try to figure out why the brake sticks, they have no choice, its habit and reflex and they have to know, even if there is no point in knowing.

Does this mean I don't think there is any point in even knowing? I guess, yes, why are we pretending we should care about something like this? And yet, as I sit here waiting for the cardiologist to come in, I realize that I'm being selfish. If this gives my dad hope or comfort, that's good, and what do I care, really, I'm here to spend time with him, absorb him, and take in as much as I can regardless of the setting or context, before I cannot do so any more.

The cardiologist comes in. I have heard he's some young hotshot they were somehow able to lure here, but I didn't expect to know him.

James, the doctor, looks at my dad, and then he looks me.

"Duuuuuuuuuuuuuuude!" James says, cruising over and giving me a big bear hug, "I didn't realize this was your dad, how crazy, right?"

"Yeah," I say, "very crazy."

And it is, because I know him of course, even if we haven't seen each other in years, and were never great friends, but also because while he was always a great guy, and he may be great at what he does, I knew him when he spent every night slumped over a three-footer too high to talk much less examine someone's heart. I also knew him when, he got pulled-over, though never charged, for DWI, and so it's hard to fathom that he can possibly be great enough to be the guy he is now.

I knew him when, and when you knew someone when you never see them as they are now, not fully anyway. That said, he seems professional enough, and caring, as he adjusts my dad's pillows, and asks him about this family history, never talking cancer, just trying to get straight on his heart, and what might be up, which is way more important at this phase.

When James is done I look at my watch and realize how late in the day it is and that I'm not just leaving the next morning, I may be leaving for good in some ways, which doesn't mean I'm not coming back, because I will come back as long as I can, but it's just not clear what kind of shape my dad will be in when I do.

Today it's the heart, and tomorrow it may be pneumonia, the cancer itself doesn't have to kill you, because there are any number of things that will be happy to kill you if given the chance.

"Duuuuuuude," James says as he gets ready to leave, "I'm almost done tonight, how about we get some coffee, or even some beers at Thirsty's before I go home. What do you say?"

"James man, I really appreciate the offer," I say, "and I really appreciate how awesome you were with my dad, but

I am going to pass all right."

"Sure, okay, how about I go grab some pizza then at Mario's and we can hang out here?"

I pause.

"Or, I can just sit here with you, keep you company, and we can just catch-up?"

I want to tell him that this isn't the time to do any of these things. That I need to just be with my dad, and not just with him, but inhaling him and taking whatever life he will give me before there isn't any more to give. But I feel like a jerk.

"Can we so this some other time?" I say.

"What," he says quizzically, "hang-out?"

He really looks confused.

"You don't want to talk at all?" he says.

"I need to be with my dad," I say too strongly, suddenly angry at James for being so obstinate, and so nice, and so focused on my dad's heart when none of it matters, when nothing matters any more. Why doesn't he get that?

"Okay," James says, clearly hurt, "next time maybe."

"Sure," I say, "thanks."

James leaves and I turn back to my dad who is sleeping. I sit down and watch him for awhile, breathing in and out, peacefully, like a baby.

63.

I have run all of my life and when it's good it can be so very good, religious, even rapturous at times, and today is one of those days, step after step, and mile after mile, just grooving, taking it all in like a vacuum and running for hours like it is the most natural thing in the world. If it is true that I continue to grow slower with age, it is also true that I care less and less about speed as I grow older, because now just feeling good outweighs anything as pedestrian as time and splits and pace.

And today I feel good, giddy really, and when I get home I feel so triumphant I want to somehow share with Kerri just how glorious the whole experience had been. But there is something wrong. She is too calm and too focused on me and how I am feeling. I know immediately it has to be something to do with my dad, but I cannot ask.

I can't even form the words. I don't want to know. So I look at her imploring to her to say anything else. Or, nothing if that's easier. And she stares at me, sad and shaken, but holding strong and willing herself to say something, which she finally does.

"They think today may be it," she says, "I'm so sorry."

We've been waiting for this, at times hopeful, at times resigned, and sometimes just mercifully wanting it to end, but if this it, and if that means that we, and this, is all done, I have no idea what to do with that.

I stare at Kerri a little longer thinking that may change something. It doesn't. I call the hospital and my mom answers.

"Hey," I say, "so…"

"He appears to have stabilized," she says. "Do you want to talk to him?"

"Of course," I say watching myself talk from across the room as the sweat on my brow and back and behind my knees forms little rivulets and tributaries that trickle towards the floor and pool around my shoes.

"H-h-hello," my dad says breathing hard, barely legible and sounding like his mom did at the end.

"Hey," I say hesitantly, but with as much enthusiasm as I can muster, "I wanted to check in, you know be a good son."

I'm not sure why I say this, I never think like this, but it is the end, or close to it and I'm fishing for something. Maybe it's that we all want to know we are loved and we did right by those we love, but don't always know how to talk to.

"Y-y-you have been a good son," he replies.

My knees buckle. I dry heave. Then I fall apart, slowly falling from some great height as a million cells implode all at once. What is it about that response? This is what I was expecting, right, or maybe it's what I was hoping for, because maybe I didn't know this. Thinking you're something doesn't make it true.

"Dad, I will call you back later," I say in a rush as I try to push out the words before the tears really start to come and he hears just how not tough I am right now.

Then I hang up and as I do it hits me, really hits me, that whatever else I think I'm thinking, or feeling, what's really happened here is the recognition that my dad may not have died today, but he will die soon because this is what death sounds like.

I try to move, pace, something, anything, but I'm too scared to move, I'm not sure anything still works. So instead I drop to my knees, just hoping to regain my equilibrium and for a moment, a long moment, I think I'm going to get away without crying, but then Kerri comes over to embrace me, and that's it.

I cry all the tears I have not, or could not, cry prior to now. I cry so hard I cannot talk, then again there is nothing to say.

64.

My father hallucinates now when he's actually awake and talks about Madagascar, and zebra meat and the hunt. Other times he talks about his friend Joe and how Joe plans to help him escape from the prison he suddenly finds himself in. He also talks about the Nazi's, telling anyone willing to listen that they are coming and we must be prepared.

It's about anger and guilt and confusion. Waking up agitated and questioning where it is we are exactly. There is oxygen debt, moans and edema. There is morphine and Atavan. And the possibility, blessedly, that he may just keep sleeping, never to wake again as his body breaks down, piece by piece, part by part, until all that remains is the hearing, and the memories, and the ever-present questions.

How did we get here? Is this real? Where and how will we end up?

"Do you think I'm getting out of the hospital?" he said to me earlier tonight during a brief stretch of lucidity.

"I don't think so, at least not any time soon," I reply, turning away to hide the tears in my eyes and the lump in my throat.

"Look at that, we're back where we started," he says before he drifts off to sleep for maybe the last time.

I watch him for a moment. He looks peaceful and I'm happy for him, though I don't know if I'm ever going to talk to him again.

You might wonder how I feel about this, but I don't know, I'm too numb to answer that question.

You then might ask again, if at this moment, right now, I think I am finally prepared for my father's death and that would be fine question to ask.

What I would tell you, again, is that I am numb, but what I would also tell you is that I'm not too numb to know there's little question that I'm prepared or ever will be.

And I know this without question for two reasons, if "reasons" is even the word I'm actually looking for.

First, there is my friend Christie and her tale about the time her sister smelled her long dead mother's perfume on some random woman on the street and then followed her for five blocks just to lose herself in it.

And second, there is the story my mom once told me about the time she took a nap while she was battling breast cancer and dreamt about taking a nap with her own mother already dead almost twenty-five years. When I asked my mom what she thought it meant, she replied, "I need a mother."

And that's all I need to know I guess. You do not forget, cannot forget, will not forget the loss of a parent no matter how much time goes by, and since I do not, cannot, and will not forget, how can I ever be prepared?

65.

"You know about palliative care, right?" my dad's friend Joe says leaning in so close to me that our noses are practically touching.

Joe is an old friend of the family who has come to visit my dad and asked me to sit with him outside in the hospital's garden so we can have a "chat."

He prides himself on being helpful. He prides himself on being provocative and saying what must be said. He apparently does not pride himself however on trimming his nose hair and as much as I am trying to concentrate on what he is saying, it is near impossible for me to pay attention to anything but the black tendrils that are poking out of his flared nostrils and looking to make a break for it.

I try to snap back to attention.

"Palliative care?" I say trying not to stare at the nose hairs that now seem to be trying to leap from his face to mine. "I'm not sure what you mean."

"What I mean," he says winking and leaning closer, so close that I imagine the nose hairs brushing my lips, "is that you can tell the nurse your father is in pain and that they can make him more comfortable by increasing his morphine."

"Do you think he is in pain?" I ask still distracted and knowing he's trying to say something without saying it, but that I just don't quite know what that is.

"That doesn't matter," he says as spittle flies onto my eye brow.

"No?"

"No," he says suddenly gripping my leg with a freakishly vice-like grip, "with enough morphine he won't have to feel anything ever again."

After he says this he leans back and crosses his legs, lacing his fingers around his left knee. He looks very satisfied with himself.

"So you think we should kill him?" I ask relieved that I have not only figured out what he was implying, but that he and his nose hair have receded from my immediate line of vision.

"Kill him," he says, "no I didn't say that, I said you could make him more comfortable. You think I'm fucking Jack Kevorkian."

I don't answer that.

66.

My father never quite wakes up again. His breathing changes from hour to hour if not moment to moment and with each change comes the sense that we know just how far long he now must be. But we don't of course, nor does anyone else it would seem. Every hour and every night appears to be the last, but they are not. He keeps breathing if nothing else and so we wait. And we are tired.

Selflessly I want him to move on because I cannot believe this is the kind of life he would remotely want, nor do I want him to suffer. Selfishly though, and unspoken, there's also part of me that wants him to move on because I need him to in so many ways. This is too hard now and has gone on too long and I just can't bear to be here like this. It's too much and on some level it feels like enough is enough.

Of course the longer he holds on the more I learn about him, and the more I learn about the things we have in common, things I suppose I know, or should have anyway. There was his fear of the suburbs and domesticity for example, that they sap if not outright destroy your creativity and energy, and how he was always in awe whenever he saw an orthodox Jew. That being a writer and an artist was not always easy for him, that it was a struggle, something that seems so obvious now. And these are good things to know. Things that allow me to flesh out what is clearly an incomplete picture of this complex man who is not much longer for this world regardless of how many breaths he continues to take.

And what about those tortured breaths rattling about in his throat? What do they represent, if anything? I imagine I could get into all sorts of spiritual type explanations that I hate and don't believe in, or at least don't want to believe in. But instead what I decide to believe as I sit there, hour after hour, time collapsing into itself until even the seconds passing feels like white noise, is that those breaths represent my dad's will to live regardless of how hopeless things could have seemed and how overwhelming this whole experience has been.

Said differently, I decide to believe that he's a tough guy right up until the end, and the breaths make it so. Does thinking this make it any easier to cope with what's going on though? No. And does thinking this help me better make sense of something that is completely senseless to me? No. In fact, as my father has grown sicker my mom has repeatedly asked if there aren't things I think my dad and I might want to discuss and sometimes when it was just me and her hanging out she would say something like "aren't there things you want to know about him?"

Though I never ask her what she thinks those things might be, I know it is his leaving that she feels I should explore before it's too late to do so. There were times when my dad mentioned the regrets he had regarding his actions towards the family and how he wished he could take them back. I suppose that these might have been openings or not so unconscious pleas by him to open the door for me. He being able to go only so far on his own, yet hoping I would push him in some way, maybe even absolve him of things done and left unsaid. But I never took the bait and I didn't ask him about his regrets and what it all meant to him and to us.

It's hard to know now why I didn't ask, sitting here in the hospital, watching him breathe and knowing we will never talk about anything again. I imagine I didn't ask because I didn't really want to know the truth, or more accurately didn't want the truth as I already knew it to be confirmed. Maybe it was more about my dad than me though, because he never really talked about such things and so I wouldn't even have known where to start.

Of course, it may be none of this, and it may be way more obvious. Maybe I just didn't want to be angry at him. What could he have said about leaving us that would have made it okay or rational or acceptable? Nothing, and if he couldn't have said anything, maybe it's better to lose someone and be left bereft and confused versus bereft and angry.

The former has to be easier to manage, doesn't it?

It's kind of funny though, even disingenuous, to even think about all this and pretend I never tried to broach this at all, because there was one time I asked him about those years.

I was home for the weekend and we went out to the quarry to pick up some rocks for a home improvement plan of his. I remember the sky was all pink and hazy and as we shoveled the rocks into a bag I watched him, still young, strong and lean, but vulnerable too, the sun softening his visage and taming his endlessly tensile forearms.

"Hey," I suddenly blurted out, heart pounding, "why did you leave when I was a kid, what we're you thinking? Were you thinking?"

This comes out in a rush, an onslaught of language, impossible to avoid, but impossible to provide an easy answer to, something I know even as I say it. There is a moment after the words come out, and they are still hanging in the air, that I feel bad for asking this. But it's just a moment, because then I think, why should I have to keep this in, buried and dormant and rotting? Why should I have to deal with it myself? Fuck you, motherfucker. And then the words are no longer hanging out there in the quickly fading evening light, and now I'm just waiting for some kind of response.

"What else could I do?" he finally says.

My dad's face crumbles as he says this, and his shoulders slump. He no longer looks vulnerable, just beaten down and weak. It's terrible and I drop it right there, never to mention any of it again. I couldn't. I didn't ever want to see him like that again, ever.

And so are there things to talk about, of course, but am I going to talk about them, no way.

67.

I am just beginning to doze off when it gets so very quiet, and while silence, intense silence like that, wouldn't normally provide me with such a jolt, this is different, because I am sitting beside my father's bed, and he has been anything but quiet.

I jump up and say "dad are you alright," addressing a man who has barely spoken in days. He does not answer, and fearing his last breath has passed I lean over him searching for any sign that I am wrong.

As I do, he breathes again. It is calmest breath I've heard all week. Then it stops, and the world stops for just a moment, and that's it, and I know no breath will follow.

What am I supposed do at such a moment? I know it's been coming and maybe even been wishing it would just a little, but then there it is, the last thing I'd ever want.

I tell the nurse and then I try to call home, but the phone is off the hook and so I go back to the house to wake everyone up and let them know, which maybe is better anyway, more personal and not so cliché.

Then we sit with him, and laugh with him, and cry with him, all of us there in the room, my mom, Kerri, Jerry and me, we sit there, as he lays there between us, his mortal shell, relaxed and unreal, no life remaining.

We escort him to the funeral home. We call people and they call us. There is a funeral. Friends and family appear as if by magic at times. And it's all a blur really.

Because that's what death looks like at first, a swirl of movement created to compensate for the sudden lack of movement death has brought and the desire not to think about what has occurred. In fact there is only one moment where I even stop to think at all.

I am standing in our dining room with Kerri, having a drink, talking to anyone who passes by, when I notice that lawn girl has come to the house and is talking to my mom. I go to excuse myself and speak to her, but when she notices me walking over she scrunches up her face and then silently puts her hand up and waves me off.

I'm caught there between Kerri, lawn girl and the fates, stuck, unable to move, unsure of what to do next, and then as I look from lawn girl to Kerri, who's not even paying attention to the exchange, and back again, I'm struck, if only briefly that we can never escape our regrets, we can adapt to them, we can try to ignore them, and we can keep moving, but we can't escape them, because something will always be there to remind us of our mistakes, failures and weaknesses. It's the way of the world and my dad may or may not have understood this before he got sick, but he certainly did at the end.

68.

There is this sense, or maybe it's a belief, even if it's not totally conscious, that whatever we are feeling when someone first dies is how we will feel from that point on, that this thing has happened, it's done and in terms of that person and our relationship to them, we remain in a static sort of position, in limbo, caught between death and life, moving in most directions, just not this one.

One night after we have come home again and sort of settled into whatever patterns existed before my dad got sick, work, shop, eat, laundry, and on and on, Kerri and I rent *Frequency*, a movie starring Dennis Quaid and Jim Caviezel.

In the movie Jim plays Dennis' son and when he was a boy, the hobby they shared together was playing with a ham radio. Dennis who is a fireman then dies in a terrible fire and Jim grows up to be a bitter, drunken cop. One night Jim pulls out the old ham radio and when he turns it on he somehow connects with his dad who is on the radio as well, albeit thirty years earlier and prior to the fire. Jim then goes on to clue Dennis in on his life, what he can look forward to and so on.

As I watch this cheese ball scene I get caught up in just how not real it is, and how we don't get to talk to our dads once they are gone. We don't get the opportunity to catch them up on all they've missed or prep them for what may still come. Nor do we get to make good and ask the questions we never got to ask.

It's not like that. It can never be like that. And what could suck more than that? As I'm thinking about all this I start to cry, first softly and quietly, then harder and louder, so hard I can't see straight. I'm practically having convulsions.

Kerri's watching me and she starts to cry as well, small tears at first, then full-on on ones, big and fat. She then goes to turn off the movie.

"What are you doing," I say between tears.

"I can't bear to watch you cry so hard," she says.

"I haven't cried this hard since before my dad died," I say, "and it feels good to be crying this hard again."

"Really?" she says.

"Really," I respond, "and I need to watch the rest of this for that reason alone."

"Fine," she says walking back to the couch.

We watch the rest of the movie in silence, and as we do, I realize yet again that even though I may be able to cry these days, it doesn't mean I don't still struggle to feel things, and this is important because here I am trying to figure out what it takes to be a writer, and like my dad my first inclination is not to dig and uncover all those horrible things that might be lurking beneath the surface, the regrets and the pain, the confusion and the sense that I never feel like I understand what everyone else seems to get about how things work.

The thing is I need to dig in if the writing is going to be honest and resonate with people. The question as always though is whether I am willing to do so.

69.

Marcus and I are at Marie's Golden Cue up on Montrose after work. He thinks I need to get out which I haven't really been doing, instead focused more on work and home, and some semblance of normalcy than actually living. I haven't even been out running. And it may be survivor guilt, exhaustion, profound sadness or a desire to do nothing after doing so much, but whatever it is, I'm sure I will get moving soon, it takes time.

Marcus doesn't want to wait though.

"You know my dad died a couple of years ago, right?" Marcus says lining-up his shot.

"Yeah," I say, "I guess I do."

"He was tough," Marcus says after missing the seven, "you know tough to talk to, not a lot of emotion or anything."

"Yeah, huh," I reply trying to focus on the fifteen.

"And since it was hard for me to talk to him," Marcus continues, "I didn't have all the answers I wanted when he died, you know?"

"Sure," I say watching the fifteen drop, and moving on to the fourteen.

"Also," Marcus continues, "I noticed that since he didn't say a lot, or you know, open himself up or anything, that maybe I wasn't so good at it either."

"Right, okay," I say watching the fourteen come to stop on the lip of the pocket.

"So, it helped me when people sort of tried to make me talk about him, you *know*," Marcus says looking at me.

It is at this moment that I finally realize that Marcus wants me to know that he is available to talk to me about my dad and whatever I'm feeling, but isn't quite capable of saying so directly.

God bless dudes.

I decide to fuck with him, a reminder that even in the midst of despondency and confusion, things go on, we can feel pleasure and laugh at things, an observation that is sad and confusing all its own.

"Hey," I say, "are you trying to ask me something, I think you are, but it's just not entirely clear to me?"

"Fuck-you," Marcus says extending his middle finger, "are you going to make me say it?"

"Yeah," I say sitting down by the table, "I think I would feel better, more loved I guess, if you could just say what is you want to say."

Of course, what I should do is tell him how much I appreciate him trying to get me to talk, that it isn't easy to know what I'm feeling, but that I do have some ideas.

"Look," I say, "I really appreciate this."

"You're not going to ask for a hug are you," he says, "because Homey don't play that."

"No, man," I say, "I just uh, I don't know, my dad sort of struggled as an artist, you know, it didn't define him, but it was a struggle, and I have been thinking about that a lot, maybe too much, because maybe I should focus more on him and what it means that he's gone and less on me and the impact his life had on how I'm living mine."

"Yeah?"

"Yeah, he wanted more you know, creating any sort of art is a wonderful thing, a fantastical thing really, but what makes someone an artist lies in the transaction, someone must receive it, and I have been wondering how much his challenges trying to achieve this had an effect on me."

"What do you mean?" Marcus says taking a seat next to me.

"I want to be a writer, not just someone who writes," I respond, suddenly, urgently, it's something I've never really said out loud, but it's clearly something I want to try on for size. I also clearly want to see how Marcus will react to it.

"That's cool," Marcus says, "so then do it, write, what's the big deal?"

"I don't know man. I really think that my dad's struggles influenced my ability to get started. The artist's life is filled with some incredibly soaring highs, and he had those, but are the highs worth the struggles, the rejection and the absolute focus required to hone your craft? To be honest, my father made it clear that he loved us, but he also made it clear that having a family prevented him from achieving the kind of single-minded determination required for success."

"Is it all about success," Marcus asks, "and does it have to be all about your father?"

Does it have to be all about my father? That's like saying does living have to be all about breathing? No, not exactly, but can you ever really separate it?

I stand up and take aim at the twelve. I tap it lightly with the cue and as the chalk dust wends its way up towards the lights I watch the twelve slowly, but surely, roll towards the side pocket and the drop, disappearing from sight.

For a long time I tried not to think about writing, something I failed to accomplish much of the time, but here, now, watching that twelve ball drop I am struck that not wanting to think about it has not allowed me to be the me I may have been. It doesn't have to be too late though, and my father's death only serves to illuminate this.

One the one hand it reminds me that no one has all the time in the world, and I have to act before it disappears. On the other hand, his death has liberated me to become whatever it is I might become, which is also sad and confusing, but real.

All that remains is the eight ball and as I go to shoot at it I notice that Marcus is just staring at me now, waiting for me to say something, anything, but not wanting to rush me. I tap the cue ball and as it rolls across the expanse of the table I catch myself thinking about the movie *Unbreakable*.

Bruce Willis has all these crazy powers, but they have been lying there hidden from him, and not just hidden, he's been holding them back, and then boom, he exposes himself to all the possibilities that are him and he's a fucking superhero.

It's all quite magical really and as the eight ball starts rolling, wavering, but sure, I start thinking about how maybe I can be that guy as well, that maybe I've been holding myself back, but that I don't have to.

And then as the eight ball drops, I think, I am that guy, and it's too bad my dad won't ever get to meet him or talk about any of this, because that's something he would have really enjoyed.

70.

After work I get on the train and take it down to the Jackson stop, passing from above the ground to under it, from Uptown to downtown.

I am heading to The Harold Washington Library with its crazy gargoyles looming on the roof and watching everyone coming in and passing by, ensuring not safety necessarily, but serving notice anyway, you will pay attention they seem to say, we are here, and we are not going anywhere, respect it.

Now whether this is a statement about Harold Washington's lingering impact on the city or the roll of books in our lives I cannot say, but both images seem important tonight.

I am going to the library because Studs Terkel is going to be there to discuss his new book *Will the Circle be Unbroken?* It's this riff on death and life and religion and everything in between, and apparently Studs decided needed to write it after his wife died.

I take my place in the audience and there he is, with his wispy silver hair and Jimmy Durante eyes. He's wearing his red-checked shirt and red socks, and he's being Studs, dropping names, talking up big government and championing everyday heroes. He's practically preaching, and I'm just flat out into it and hanging on every word. I mean I'm totally sold, I have found religion and the religion is Studs.

Studs then starts talking about how writing about death is really just writing about life because to talk about death you have to talk about life. All sorts of people he says told him he had to write this book, but what we don't realize is that he needed to write this book because given his wife's passing writing it was a "tonic" for him.

And I know exactly what he is trying to say. We may all experience loss, but when we do we all need to grieve in our own way. Studs is a historian, a writer and a raconteur and so how else was he supposed to cope, but to sit back, talk to his people and write about death?

After Studs is done, I drift back underground and back to the train and home. I grab my running shoes and head out to the lake and at first I am stiff and winded from all the time off, my form over the place, no rhythm or synchronicity.

But soon enough, I'm loose and floating along. The clutter from the day dissipates, and then it's me and Studs and my dad and all the stuff that has gone down.

There I was rushing home one Friday afternoon so I could call my dad to find out if the doctors had figured out why his blood was looking so fucked-up, and then he tells me that as it turns out they had found something. And now here we are not even eighteen months later and he's not here and we have to figure out how to live with that.

Of course, what so crazy and confusing, and maybe even wonderful is that even as people die and even as we try to figure out how to grieve them good things still happen along the way. Babies are born. And there are amazing sunsets. You get to see Studs Terkel and run along a lake. And you laugh again. You go on somehow and not just because you have to, but because everything goes on and life does not wait until you are ready to do so no how matter how much you want to fight it.

Soon enough I am home and when I get inside, I sit down, I take off my running shoes and I start to write.